ISAAC BABEL

# RED
# CAVALRY

Translated from the Russian
by Boris Dralyuk

PUSHKIN PRESS

LONDON

Pushkin Press
71–75 Shelton Street, London WC2H 9JQ

English translation © Boris Dralyuk 2014

*Red Cavalry* was originally published as
*Конармия* in Russia in 1926

This translation first published by Pushkin Press in 2014

ISBN 978 1 782270 93 5

Frontispiece: Isaac Babel

Set in 10 on 13.5 Monotype Baskerville by Tetragon, London

Proudly printed and bound in Great Britain by TJ International,
Padstow, Cornwall on Munken Premium White 90gsm

www.pushkinpress.com

# CONTENTS

# TRANSLATOR'S FOREWORD

The stories that make up the *Red Cavalry* cycle, which chronicle the narrator's stint as a correspondent in the Polish–Soviet War of 1919–20, originally appeared in various journals and newspapers. They were first published as a stand-alone collection in 1926. Babel continued to edit the cycle for subsequent editions, replacing individual words and excising phrases, sentences and even entire passages. Some of these excisions are clearly the result of censorship, while others may have been motivated by changes in Babel's style. Editors and censors introduced further changes after Babel's rehabilitation in the 1950s. These alterations, and the failure of earlier translators to take stock of them, are discussed in detail in Charles B. Timmer's article 'Translation and Censorship' (*Miscellanea Slavica: To Honour the Memory of Jan M. Meijer* [Amsterdam: Rodopi, 1983], pp. 443–68). They are also meticulously chronicled in Christopher Luck's annotated edition of the Russian text, titled *Babel: Red Cavalry* (London: Bristol Classical Press/Duckworth, 1994). In preparing this translation I have relied heavily on Timmer's and Luck's work, as well as on Timothy D. Sergay's review essay of Peter Constantine's translation of Babel's complete prose,

7

'Isaac Babel's Life in English: The Norton *Complete Babel* Reconsidered' (*Translation and Literature* 15:2 [Autumn 2006], pp. 238–53). I owe a great debt to these men, as well as to many other scholars of Babel's work; they have helped me avoid several potential pitfalls and correct inaccuracies that had crept into previous translations. It would be unethical of me not to acknowledge the pioneering and inventive work of translators who have tackled the *Cavalry* before me, including Nadia Helstein, Walter Morison, Andrew R. MacAndrew, David McDuff and Peter Constantine, among others. I have learnt from all of them.

I chose to base my translation on the first edition of *Red Cavalry* (1926). I did not feel it prudent to judge which omissions and changes in later editions were Babel's own and which were the work of censors, even when the answer was fairly clear. Instead, I've tried to present a rendition of the cycle as the young Babel first envisioned it. This is the work of a daring young artist—a book "full of courage and crude joy", to quote the narrator's description of *The Red Cavalryman* newspaper, and still reverberating with the terror of battle. The only exception is the story 'Argamak', which was appended to the cycle in 1933, having appeared in a journal in 1932; it is included here as a postscript. My choice of a particular edition of the original text, however, should not imply that I have been slavishly literal to that text; I have taken some liberties in order to capture Babel's tone, as I perceive it. Delicate modulations of tone are as essential to the cycle's impact as its imagery. In order to illustrate the kinds of liberties I have taken, I would like to offer an example that I originally included in a short essay for the journal *In Other Words*.

In the space of a few lines, Babel shifts from one register to another, from lyricism to brutal grittiness. A translator who cannot grasp the subtle indicators of these shifts in the original, and who can't discern an original image from a fixed turn of phrase, is liable to make a tonal mistake. Here is a sample paragraph from my translation of 'The Catholic Church in Novograd', in which our narrator drinks rum with a Polish priest's assistant and reflects on the seductive charms of the Catholic faith: "I was drinking rum with him. The spirit of a mysterious way of life still flickered beneath the ruins of the priest's house, and its insidious temptations weakened me. O crucifixes as tiny as a courtesan's amulets, the parchment of papal bulls, and the satin of women's letters worn thin in the blue silk of waistcoats!" In rendering this passage I felt I had to preserve the flowing lyricism of the original, and I worked hard on the sound texture (e.g. "amulets" instead of the more literal "talismans", in order to avoid a cluster of sibilants). Other translators have rendered the word used to describe the state of the letters—*istlevshikh*—more or less literally, as "mouldering" or "that had rotted", but this is a shade too ghoulish, and isn't true to the lyrical tone. If one takes a moment to imagine what Babel's narrator imagines—the romance of this decadent "way of life"—one can conjure the fragile letters before one's eyes, feel their texture; they have been "worn thin" by friction and sweat. Here, Babel has waxed romantic. Throughout the cycle, Babel uses the same adjective to describe things ranging from "decayed wadding" and "rotten hay" to an old rebbe's "withered fingers". Context is everything. There's plenty of brutality in these stories; it derives its effect from the beguiling lyricism that surrounds it.

Place names are exceedingly difficult to deal with in translation, especially when the places in question lie in Eastern and Central Europe. A single town—say, what is known today as Lviv—is bound in layers of toponyms: in this case the Polish "Lwów", the Russian "Lvov", the German "Lemberg" and so on. Babel's narrator, Lyutov, is a Jew born and raised in the Russian Empire who finds himself in hostile, heavily Polonized terrain as a Soviet war correspondent. He consistently refers to all the places he encounters using their Russian and Russified appellations. In this translation I have decided to use Polish names for places that were absorbed into the Habsburg Empire during the three partitions of the Polish–Lithuanian Commonwealth in the late eighteenth century; the names of regions that were absorbed into the Russian Empire are rendered in transliterated Russian. Lyutov treats the Zbrucz River as a cultural boundary between Soviet and Polish land. Clearly, the sense of a cultural barrier, which shifts uneasily beneath one's feet, is far more important to Babel than topographic fidelity; he famously moves the Zbrucz quite a bit to the east in order to have Lyutov cross the river into Novograd-Volynsk, which actually lies on the Słucz (now Sluch). Those interested in Babel's distortions of geography and military history may consult Norman Davies's article 'Izaak Babel's *Konarmiya* Stories, and the Polish–Soviet War, 1919–20' (*Modern Languages Review* 67:4 [1972], pp. 845–57), as well as H.T. Willetts's translation of Babel's *1920 Diary*, edited, annotated and introduced by Carol J. Avins (New Haven: Yale University Press, 1995). I have chosen to use the borders established by the Third Partition of 1795 as a symbolic linguistic boundary in my translation. Many of the places mentioned in this cycle now belong to the independent nations of Ukraine, Poland, Belarus and Lithuania, and I provide the standard contemporary rendering of each toponym in a short appendix. The names of Cracow, Warsaw and Moscow are given in their traditional English forms.

It has been an honour and a pleasure to work with Adam Freudenheim, Bryan Karetnyk, Gesche Ipsen and the team at Pushkin Press. I must thank Robert Chandler, without whom this project would not have been possible, and Maria Bloshteyn, whose encouraging feedback and sparkling wit reassured me whenever my confidence faltered—which is to say, at nearly every step. I owe a special thanks to my friend and colleague, Roman Koropeckyj, expert in all things Polish and Ukrainian. Most importantly, I am grateful to Kotrina Kajokaite, my partner and inspiration, and to my mother, Anna Glazer, whose faultless Odessan ear guided my hand.

# RED CAVALRY

(1926)

# CROSSING THE ZBRUCZ

THE SIXTH DIVISION commander reported that Novograd-Volynsk was taken today at dawn. The staff has moved out of Krapivno and our transport sprawls in a noisy rearguard along the highway that runs from Brest to Warsaw and was built on the bones of peasant men by Nicholas the First.

Fields of scarlet poppies blossom around us, a midday breeze plays in the yellowing rye and virgin buckwheat rises on the horizon like the wall of a distant monastery. The quiet Volyn bends. Volyn recedes from us into the pearly mist of birch groves and creeps into the flowery hills, its feeble arms getting tangled in thickets of hops. An orange sun rolls across the sky like a severed head, a gentle light glitters in the ravines of clouds and the banners of sunset flutter over our heads. The scent of yesterday's blood and dead horses seeps into the evening coolness. The blackened Zbrucz roars, twisting the foamy knots of its rapids. The bridges are destroyed and we are fording the river. A stately moon lies on the waves. The horses sink up to their backs and sonorous streams trickle between hundreds of horses' legs. Someone is drowning, loudly disparaging the Mother of God. The river is strewn with the black squares of carts, filled with rumbling, whistling and songs that thunder over snakes of moonlight and glistening pits.

Late at night we arrive in Novograd. In my assigned billet I find a pregnant woman, along with two red-haired, thin-necked Jews; a third Jew is sleeping, huddled up against the wall with a blanket over his head. In my assigned room I find two ransacked wardrobes, scraps of women's fur coats on the floor, human excrement and shards of the sacred plate that Jews use once a year—on Passover.

"Clean this up," I say to the woman. "You live in filth, hosts…"

The two Jews spring into action. They jump around on felt soles, picking debris off the floor. They jump silently, monkey-like, like a Japanese circus act, their necks swelling and swivelling. They spread a torn feather mattress on the floor and I lie down, facing the wall, next to the third, sleeping Jew. Fearful poverty closes in above my bed.

Silence has killed everything off, and only the moon, with its blue hands clasping its round, sparkling, carefree head, tramps about under the window.

I stretch my numbed legs. I lie on the torn feather mattress and fall asleep. I dream of the Sixth Division commander. He's chasing the brigade commander on a heavy stallion and plants two bullets in his eyes. The bullets pierce the brigade commander's head, and both his eyes fall to the ground.

"Why'd you turn the brigade back?" Savitsky, the Sixth Division commander, shouts at the wounded man—and here I wake up, because the pregnant woman's fingers are fumbling over my face.

"Pan,"[1] she says to me. "You're screaming in your sleep, thrashing around. I'll make your bed in the other corner, because you're shoving my papa…"

She raises her skinny legs and round belly off the floor and removes the blanket from the huddled sleeper. It's a dead old man, flat on his back. His gullet is ripped out, his face is hacked in two, and blue blood sits in his beard like a hunk of lead.

"Pan," says the Jewess, giving the feather mattress a shake. "The Poles were slashing him and he kept begging them, 'Kill me in the back yard so my daughter doesn't see me die.' But they did it their way—he died in this room, thinking of me… And now you tell me," the woman said suddenly with terrible force, "you tell me where else in this whole world you'll find a father like my father…"

*Novograd-Volynsk, July 1920*

# THE CATHOLIC CHURCH IN
# NOVOGRAD

YESTERDAY I TOOK a report to the military commissar, who was staying at the house of a priest that had run off. In the kitchen I met Pani Eliza, the Jesuit's housekeeper. She gave me amber tea with biscuits. Her biscuits smelt like the crucifixion. They contained the sly sap and sweet-scented fury of the Vatican.

The bells in the church next door were roaring, set into motion by the maddened ringer. The evening was full of midsummer stars. Pani Eliza, shaking her attentive grey tresses, kept slipping me biscuits, and I took pleasure in the Jesuit food.

The old Polish woman called me "Pan", grey old men with ossified ears stood to attention near the threshold, and somewhere in the serpentine twilight a monk's cassock was fluttering. The *pater* ran off, but he left his assistant—Pan Romuald.

A snuffling eunuch with the body of a giant, Romuald addressed us respectfully, as "comrades". He'd draw a yellow finger across the map, tracing the circles of the Polish rout. Overcome with raspy enthusiasm, he'd recount his fatherland's wounds. Let gentle oblivion engulf all memory of Romuald, who betrayed us without pity and was shot dead in passing. But that evening his narrow cassock flitted at every door-curtain, furiously sweeping all the roads and grinning at anyone who wanted vodka. That evening the monk's shadow tailed me relentlessly. He would have made bishop, Pan Romuald—if he hadn't been a spy.

I was drinking rum with him. The spirit of a mysterious way of life still flickered beneath the ruins of the priest's house, and its insidious temptations weakened me. O crucifixes as tiny as a courtesan's amulets, the parchment of papal bulls, and the satin of women's letters worn thin in the blue silk of waistcoats!…

I can see you from here, faithless monk in a lilac robe— your hands swollen, your soul as tender and pitiless as the soul of a cat; I see the wounds of your God, oozing seed, a sweet-smelling poison that intoxicates virgins.

We were drinking rum, waiting for the military commissar to return from headquarters, but he wouldn't show. Romuald dropped down in a corner and fell asleep. He sleeps and trembles, and outside the window the garden path shimmers beneath the black passion of the sky. Thirsty roses sway in the darkness. Bursts of green lightning flare in the church's domes. A naked corpse sprawls at the foot of the slope. Moonbeams stream across the dead legs jutting wide apart.

There's your Poland, there's the haughty grief of the Commonwealth! A violent intruder, I spread a louse-ridden mattress in a temple abandoned by the clergyman and rest my head on folios full of printed hosannas to His Excellency, the illustrious chief of state, Józef Piłsudski.[1]

Hordes of beggars roll on to your ancient cities, O Poland, and a song calling all serfs to unite thunders above them—and woe to you, Commonwealth, woe to you, Prince Radziwiłł, and to you, Prince Sapieha, who rose for but an hour!...[2]

My commissar doesn't show. I look for him at head-quarters, in the garden, in the church. The church gates are open; I go in and am met by the sudden glare of two silver skulls on the lid of a broken coffin. In terror I rush downstairs, to the crypt. An oak staircase leads from there to the altar. And I see a multitude of lights darting high above, up in the very dome. I see the commissar, the chief of the Special Section, and Cossacks with candles in their hands. They respond to my weak cry and lead me out of the basement.

The skulls, which turn out to be carvings on the church bier, no longer scare me, and we all continue the search, because this was a search, which began after piles of military uniforms were discovered in the priest's rooms.

Sparkling with the horses' muzzles embroidered on our cuffs, whispering and rattling with our spurs, we go round the echoing building with guttering wax in our hands. Mothers of God, studded with precious stones, follow us with their pink, mouse-like pupils, flames pulse in our fingers, and rectangular shadows writhe on the statues of St Peter, St Francis and St Vincent, on their rosy cheeks and curly beards coloured with carmine.

We go round and search. Ivory buttons spring beneath our fingers; icons that are split down the middle move apart, revealing vaults in caves that blossom with mould. This temple is ancient and full of secrets. Its glossy walls conceal secret passages, niches and trapdoors that swing open without making a sound.

O foolish priest, who hung the bras of his parishioners on the nails in the Saviour's hands! In the Holy of Holies we found a suitcase stuffed with gold coins, a morocco-leather bag of banknotes and Parisian jewellers' cases with emerald rings.

Later we counted the money in the commissar's room. Columns of gold, carpets of banknotes, a gusty wind blowing on the candle flames, the crow-like bewilderment in Pani Eliza's eyes, Romuald's thunderous laughter and the endless roar of the bells struck by Pan Robacki, the maddened ringer.

"Away," I told myself. "Away from these winking Madonnas deceived by soldiers…"

# A LETTER

HERE IS A LETTER HOME, dictated to me by Kurdyukov, a boy in our detachment. It doesn't deserve oblivion. I copied it out, without any embellishment, and pass it on word for word, in accordance with the truth.

*Dear mama Yevdokiya Fyodorovna. In the first lines of this letter I hasten to inform you that, thank the good Lord, I'm alive and well, which same I'd like to hear from you. And I bow low before you, my white brow on the damp earth…* (There follows a list of kith, kin, godparents. We'll omit it and proceed to the second paragraph.)

*Dear mama Yevdokiya Fyodorovna Kurdyukova. I hasten to write that I'm in Comrade Budyonny's Red Cavalry,[1] and so is my godfather Nikon Vasilich, who is at present a Red Hero. He took me to work for him, in the Polit-Department's detachment, where we distribute pamphlets and newspapers along the front—the Moscow Central Committee's Izvestiya, the Moscow Pravda and our own merciless paper The Red Cavalryman, which every frontline fighter here wants to read all the way through, because then they get the heroic spirit and hack the damn Polacks to pieces, and I get along here at Nikon Vasilich's real fine.*

*Dear mama Yevdokiya Fyodorovna. Send whatever you can spare. I'm asking—slaughter our speckled boar and put together a parcel, send it to Comrade Budyonny's Polit-Department, make it out to Vasily Kurdyukov. I lay myself down every night without eating, without any clothes, so it's mighty cold. Write me a letter about my Styopa—he alive, dead? I'm asking—look after him and write me about him. Is he still clipping like he used to, and also about the mange on his front legs, and is he shod? I'm asking, dear mama Yevdokiya Fyodorovna, keep washing his front legs with soap all the time—the soap I left behind the icons—and if papa's used it up, buy some more in Krasnodar so God don't abandon you. And I can tell you that the land's plenty poor here. The peasants run to the woods with their horses, hiding out from our Red eagles. There's not much wheat, you know, and it's awful small—good for a laugh. Those with land, they sow rye and oats. Hops grow on sticks in these parts, so they come out very neat—and everyone makes moonshine.*

*In the second lines of this letter, I hasten to describe about papa, how he chopped down my brother Fyodor Timofeich Kurdyukov a year back. Our Red Brigade, under Comrade Pavlichenko, was advancing on the city of Rostov, when there was treason in our ranks. And papa was with Denikin[2] at the time, a company commander. The people that saw him back then, they said he had medals all over him, like under the old regime. And on account of this treason, all of us were taken prisoner, and papa caught sight of brother Fyodor Timofeich. And papa took to slashing Fyodor with a sabre, calling him a worthless hide, red dog, son of a bitch, and all sorts of things, and he slashed him till it was dark, till Fyodor Timofeich was gone. I wrote you a letter then, how your Fedya is lying without a cross. But papa, he caught me with the letter and he said, "You're your mother's sons, you take after that whore—I filled her belly up once, I'll do it again—my life's ruined—I'll kill off my own seed for the sake of justice," and all sorts of things. I suffered at his hands like the saviour Jesus Christ. Only soon I got away from papa and found my way to my unit, under Comrade Pavlichenko. And our brigade received orders to go to the city of Voronezh for reinforcements, and so we got reinforcements there, along with horses, cartridge pouches, revolvers and everything we had coming to us. As for Voronezh, I can describe about it, dear mama Yevdokiya Fyodorovna, that it's a real fine town, probably a trifle bigger than Krasnodar—the people are mighty handsome, and the river's fit for bathing. They gave us two pounds of bread a day, half a pound of meat, and proper sugar, so that when we'd get up we'd drank sweet tea, and we'd have the same in the evening so we forgot about hunger, and for lunch I'd go to brother Semyon Timofeich's for pancakes or goose, and then I'd lie down for a rest. At the time the whole regiment wanted Semyon Timofeich for a commander, on account of how wild he is, and so Comrade Budyonny gave the order, and Semyon got two stallions, proper clothes, a whole separate cart for this and that, and the Order of the Red Banner—and they gave me special consideration as his brother. From then on, say some neighbour treats you badly—Semyon Timofeich can cut him right down, just like that. Then we gave chase to General Denikin, and we cut them down by the thousands and drove them into the Black Sea, only papa was nowhere to be found—and Semyon Timofeich looked for him all over the front, on account of he missed our brother Fyodor. But you know full well, dear mama, about papa and how stubborn he is—so what did he do? He went and dyed his beard from red to black and holed up in the town of Maykop, in civilian clothes, so that nobody there had a clue that he'd been as much a constable as could be under the old regime. But the truth, it'll always out. Godfather Nikon Vasilich happened to see him in some local's hut and wrote a letter to Semyon Timofeich about it. So we get on our horses and ride two hundred versts[3]—myself, brother Senka and some boys from the village what were willing.*

*And what did we see in this Maykop? We saw that the rear don't feel a whit for the front, that there's treason all over the place and that it's full of yids, like under the old regime. And Semyon Timofeich got into a fine quarrel with the yids in Maykop, who didn't want to hand papa over and put him in prison under lock and key, saying an order came down from Comrade Trotsky about not hacking prisoners up, we'll judge him ourselves, don't get sore, he'll get his. But Semyon Timofeich proved that he's regimental commander and has every Order of the Red Banner from Comrade Budyonny, and he threatened to cut down anyone who stood up for papa and wouldn't hand him over, and the boys from the village did a little threatening too. Soon as Semyon Timofeich got papa, they set to whipping him and lined all the fighting boys up in the yard, in proper military order. And then Senka splashed water on papa Timofei Rodionych's beard, and dye came dripping off the beard. And Senka asked Timofei Rodionych:*

"Well, papa, does it feel good, being in my hands?"

"No," said papa. "It's bad."

Then Senka asked:

"And Fedya, when you were slashing at him, was it good for him, in your hands?"

"No," said papa. "It was bad for Fedya."

Then Senka asked:

"And did you think, papa, that it'd be bad for you?"

"No," said papa. "I didn't think it'd be bad for me."

Then Senka turned to the people and said:

"Well, I think that if yours ever get ahold of me, there won't be any mercy. And now, papa, we'll finish you off…"

And Timofei Rodionych commenced cursing Senka—mother this, Mother of God that—and smacking Senka in the face, and Semyon Timofeich sent me away from the yard, so I can't, dear mama Yevdokiya Fyodorovna, describe to you how they finished papa off, seeing how I was sent away from the yard.

After that we had a stop in the city of Novorossiysk. Of this town I can say that there's no land beyond it, only water, the Black Sea, and we stayed there right up until May, when we set out for the Polish front, and now we're giving the Polacks real hell…

I remain your dear son Vasily Timofeich Kurdyukov. Mama, look after Styopka so God don't abandon you.

That's Kurdyukov's letter, not a word of it altered. When I'd finished, he took the paper covered with writing and stuck it inside his shirt, next to his naked body.

"Kurdyukov," I asked the boy, "was your father bad?"

"My father was a dog," he said grimly.

"Is your mother any better?"

"Mother's proper. If you want—here's our folk…"

He handed me a creased photograph. It showed Timofei Kurdyukov, a broad-shouldered constable with his official cap and a combed beard, rigid, with high cheekbones, and with a sparkling gaze in his colourless, senseless eyes. Next to him, in a bamboo armchair, glimmered a tiny peasant woman in an untucked blouse, with sickly pale, timid features. And against the wall, against this pitiful provincial photographic background, with its flowers and doves, hulked two boys— monstrously huge, dumb, broad-faced, goggle-eyed and frozen as if on drill: the two Kurdyukov brothers—Fyodor and Semyon.

# THE CHIEF OF THE REMOUNT SERVICE

T HE WHOLE VILLAGE is whining. The cavalry's tram-
pling the grain and changing horses. The cavalrymen
are swapping their wretched nags for workhorses. No one's
to blame. Without horses there's no army.

But knowing this doesn't make the peasants feel any
better. The peasants crowd around headquarters and won't
budge.

Behind them, on ropes, they drag jibbing old hacks whose
weak legs slip and skid. The peasant men have been deprived
of their breadwinners; sensing a bitter courage welling up
inside them and aware that it won't last long, they hurry to rail
hopelessly at the authorities, at God, at their miserable fates.

Zh——, the chief of staff, stands on the porch in full
uniform. Shielding his inflamed eyelids, he listens to the
peasants' complaints, evidently paying attention. But this
attention of his is nothing more than a ploy. Like any well-
trained and overworked employee, he's able to halt the
workings of his brain altogether during vacant minutes of
existence. In these few minutes of blissful senselessness our
chief of staff overhauls his worn-out machine.

And so it is this time around, with the peasants.

To the soothing accompaniment of their disjointed and desperate din, Zh—— observes, from the sidelines, the soft jostling in his brain that heralds purity and power of thought. Arriving at the proper break, he seizes the final peasant sob, snarls authoritatively and steps back into headquarters to work.

This time he didn't even have to snarl. Suddenly Dyakov, a former circus athlete and now chief of the Remount Service—a red-skinned, grey-moustached fellow with a black cloak and silver stripes on his red Cossack trousers—came galloping up to the porch on his fiery Anglo-Arabian.

"The Father's blessing to all honest bastards!" he shouted, reining in his steed at full gallop, and at that very moment a mangy nag—one of the horses the Cossacks had swapped—keeled over right under his stirrups.

"Look there, Comrade Commander!" a peasant howled, slapping himself on his trousers. "Look—that there's what your boys hand our boys… You ever see a thing like that? Try farming on that…"

"For this steed," Dyakov began, distinctly and weightily. "For this steed, my venerable friend, you are fully entitled to receive fifteen thousand roubles from the Remount Service, and if this steed were livelier, well, that being the case, then, my beloved friend, you'd receive twenty thousand roubles from the Remount Service. Now, however, the steed fell down—but that's no matter. If the steed falls and gets back up, it's a steed; if, to put it another way, it doesn't get up, then it's no steed. But this fine little filly, well, I say she'll get up for me…"

"Oh, lordy lord, mother gracious!" the peasant threw up his hands. "How's she supposed to get up, the poor thing... Poor thing'll croak for sure..."

"You're insulting the steed, brother," Dyakov responded with deep conviction. "Brother, you're downright blaspheming." He deftly swung his statuesque athlete's body from the saddle. All splendid and deft, as if he were on the stage, he straightened his magnificent legs, which were gartered by belts at the knees, and approached the dying animal. It stared sadly at Dyakov with its deep, grim eye, licked some invisible command off his crimson palm—and suddenly the exhausted horse felt an onrush of power flowing from this grey-haired, vigorous and dashing Romeo. Weaving her snout in the air, her tottering legs slipping beneath her, the nag sensed the whip impatiently, imperiously tickling her belly and slowly, carefully rose to her feet. And we all saw a thin wrist in a flowing sleeve pat the dirty mane and a whip cling to the bleeding flank with a whine. Trembling all over, the nag stood on her four legs, never taking her dog-like, fearful, loving eyes off Dyakov.

"So it's a steed," Dyakov said to the peasant, and added softly, "and you were bellyaching, my friend..."

Tossing his reins to his orderly, the chief of the Remount Service took all four porch steps in one stride and, with a flap of his opera cloak, disappeared into headquarters.

*Belyov, July 1920*

the flock and corpulent infants rocked in cradles suspended from the straight trunks of palm trees. The brown rags of Franciscan monks surrounded a cradle. The crowd of magi was carved with glittering bald spots and wrinkles as bloody as wounds. Within the crowd flickered the foxy grin of Leo XIII's hag-like little face, and the Novograd priest himself, telling the beads of a Chinese carved rosary with one hand, blessed the newborn Jesus with the other.

For five months Apolek, ensconced in his wooden seat, crept along the walls, along the dome and through the gallery.

"You have a passion for familiar faces, my beloved Pan Apolek," the priest once remarked, recognizing himself in one of the magi and Pan Romuald in the baptist's severed head. He smiled, the old *pater*, and sent a glass of brandy up to the artist, who was working under the dome.

Then Apolek completed the Last Supper and the stoning of Mary Magdalene. One Sunday he uncovered the decorated walls. The eminent citizens the priest had invited recognized Janek, the lame convert, in the apostle Paul, and in Mary Magdalene—the Jewish girl Elka, daughter of unknown parents and mother of many a stray. The eminent citizens demanded that the profane images be covered up. The priest brought down threats upon the blasphemer. But Apolek did not cover the decorated walls.

So began the unprecedented war between the all-mighty body of the Catholic Church on the one hand, and the care-free icon-dauber on the other. It lasted three decades—a war as merciless as a Jesuit's passion. The incident nearly made the meek reveller into the founder of a new heresy. And he would surely have proved the most baffling and ridiculous warrior that the Church of Rome had faced in all its tortuous and turbulent history—a warrior wandering the earth in blissful drunkenness with two white mice under his shirt and a set of the finest brushes in his pocket.

"Fifteen złotys for the Mother of God, twenty-five złotys for the holy family and fifty złotys for the Last Supper depicting all of the customer's relatives. For ten złotys extra, the customer's enemy can be depicted as Judas Iscariot," Apolek announced to the neighbouring peasants after he was driven out of the temple.

There was no shortage of orders. And when the commission from the bishop of Zhitomir, summoned by the Novograd priest's frantic missives, finally arrived the next year, they found these monstrous family portraits—sacrilegious, naive and vivid, like the flowering of a tropical garden—in the most run-down and foul-smelling huts. Josephs with grey hair parted in the middle, pomaded Jesuses, multiparous village Marys with knees set wide apart—these icons hung in the red corners, surrounded by wreaths of paper flowers.

"He has promoted you to sainthood while you still live!" exclaimed the vicar of Dubno and Novo-Konstantinov, responding to the crowd that had gathered to defend Apolek. "He has surrounded you with the unutterable trappings of sanctity—you, who have fallen thrice into the sin of disobedience, you moonshiners, ruthless usurers, makers of false weights and sellers of your own daughters' innocence!"

"Your Holiness," responded the hobbling Witold, receiver of stolen goods and cemetery watchman. "Who's to say where the all-merciful Lord God sees the truth? How could we ignorant folk know that? And isn't there more truth in the paintings of Pan Apolek, who flatters our pride, than in your words, full of scorn and a master's wrath?…"

The crowd's whoops had the vicar on the run. The people's state of mind in the surrounding towns threatened the churchmen's safety. The artist invited to replace Apolek didn't dare to paint over Elka and lame Janek. They can be seen even now in the bye-altar of the Novograd church: Janek-Paul, a timorous cripple with a ragged black beard, a village apostate, and her, the harlot of Magdala, sickly and crazed, with a dancing body and sunken cheeks.

The battle with the priest lasted three decades. Then the Cossack flood drove the old monk from his fragrant, stony nest, and Apolek—O the vicissitudes of fate!—took up residence in Pani Eliza's kitchen. And here I am, a momentary guest, drinking the wine of his evening talks.

Talks—about what? About the romantic days of the Polish gentry, about the furious fanaticism of women, about the artist Luca della Robbia and about the family of the carpenter from Bethlehem.

"I have something to tell the Pan Clerk…" Apolek informs me mysteriously before supper.

"Yes," I say. "Yes, Apolek, I'm listening…"

But the church lay brother, Pan Robacki—stern and grey, bony and big-eared—is sitting too close. He hangs up before us faded canvases of silence and hostility.

"I have to tell the Pan," whispers Apolek, leading me aside, "that Jesus, son of Mary, was wed to Deborah, a Jerusalem maiden of common birth…"

"*Oj, ten człowiek!*"[2] Pan Robacki cries in despair. "*Ten człowiek* won't die in his own bed… *Tego człowieka*, folks will do him in…"

"After supper," Apolek rustles in a disappointed voice. "After supper, if it pleases the Pan Clerk…"

It pleases me. Kindled by the start of Apolek's story, I pace the kitchen and await the promised hour. Outside the window, night has descended like a black column. Outside the window, the dark, living garden has turned numb with cold. The road to the church flows like a milky, sparkling stream beneath the moon. The land is draped with a murky radiance, and necklaces of glowing fruits hang on the bushes. The scent of lilies is pure and strong, like alcohol. This fresh poison bites into the fatty, roiling breath of the stove and deadens the resinous stuffiness of the spruce scattered around the kitchen.

Wearing a pink bow and threadbare pink trousers, Apolek potters about in his corner like a gentle, graceful animal. His table is smeared with glue and paint. The old man works with minute, frequent movements. His corner emits the quietest of melodic drumbeats. Old Gottfried is tapping it out with his trembling fingers. The blind man sits motionless in the yellow and oily glare of the lamp. Bowing his bald forehead, he listens to the endless music of his blindness and the muttering of Apolek, his eternal friend.

"…And what the priests and the Evangelist Mark and the Evangelist Matthew tell you, Pan—it isn't true… But the truth can be revealed to the Pan Clerk, and for fifty marks I'm ready to make a portrait of the Pan in the guise of the blessed Francis, on a background of greenery and sky. He was a very simple saint, Pan Francis. And if the Pan Clerk has a bride in Russia… Women love the blessed Francis, although not all women, Pan…"

And so, in a corner smelling of spruce, began the story of Jesus' marriage to Deborah. This girl had a bridegroom, according to Apolek. Her bridegroom was a young Israelite who sold elephant tusks. But Deborah's wedding night ended in confusion and tears. The woman was gripped with fear when she saw her husband approaching her bed. Hiccups puffed out her throat. She threw up everything she had eaten at the wedding feast. Shame fell upon Deborah, upon her father, her mother and all her kin. Her bridegroom left her, jeering, and summoned all the guests. And so Jesus, seeing the anguish of the woman who yearned for her husband and feared him, put on the newlywed's garb and, full of compassion, united with Deborah, lying in her vomit. Then she went out to the guests, exulting noisily and slyly averting her gaze, like a woman proud of her fallenness. And only Jesus stood to the side. A deathly perspiration broke out over his body; the bee of sorrow stung his heart. He left the banquet hall, unseen by anyone, and withdrew to the desert country east of Judea, where John awaited him. And Deborah brought forth her first-born…

"Where is he, then?" I cried.

"The priests hid him," Apolek pronounced with significance, raising a light, chilly finger to his drunkard's nose.

"Pan Artist," Robacki suddenly cried, rising out of the darkness, his grey ears twitching. "*Co wy mówicie?*[3] That's unthinkable…"

"*Tak, tak,*" Apolek cringed and grabbed Gottfried. "*Tak, tak, Panie…*"[4]

He dragged the blind man towards the door, but paused on the threshold and beckoned me with his finger.

"Blessed Francis," he whispered, winking, "with a bird on his sleeve, a dove or a goldfinch, whatever pleases the Pan Clerk…"

And then he disappeared with the blind and eternal friend.

"Oh, what foolishness!" pronounced Robacki, the church lay brother. "*Ten człowiek* won't die in his own bed…"

Pan Robacki opened his mouth wide and yawned like a cat. I said good night and set off for home, to my pillaged Jews.

A homeless moon drifted about the town. And I walked along with her, nursing impossible dreams and discordant songs.

## THE ITALIAN SUN

YESTERDAY I AGAIN sat in Pani Eliza's rooms, beneath a hot wreath of green spruce branches. I sat near the warm, live, grumbling stove and then walked home in the dead of night. Down at the precipice the noiseless Zbrucz rolled a dark, glassy wave. My soul, suffused with the wearisome drunkenness of yearning, smiled to no one in particular, and my imagination, a blind, happy woman, swirled before me like a summertime fog.

It seemed to me that the charred town—the broken columns and the hooks of wicked old women's fingers sticking from the earth—had been raised up into the air, as snug and fanciful as a dream. The naked brilliance of the moon bathed it with an inexhaustible force. The damp mould of the ruins bloomed like a marble bench in an opera. And I waited with an anxious soul for Romeo to step out from behind the clouds, a satin Romeo singing of love while a glum electrician stands in the wings with his finger on the moon's off-switch.

Blue roads ran past me like streams of milk, flowing from many breasts. Walking home, I dreaded meeting Sidorov, my neighbour, who would drape the hairy paw of his misery over me at night. Luckily, on this night, rent by the milk of the moon, Sidorov didn't utter a word. He wrote, surrounded by books. A humpbacked candle—the sinister bonfire of dreamers—smoked on the table. I sat off to the side, dozing, dreams prancing around me like kittens. And it wasn't until late at night that I was awakened by an orderly who had come to summon Sidorov to headquarters. They left together. I then ran over to the table where Sidorov had been writing and leafed through the books. There was a teach-yourself-Italian course, a print of the Roman Forum and a plan of the city of Rome. The plan was all marked up with crosses and dots. My vague drunkenness fell from me. I leant over a sheet covered with writing and, with a sinking heart, wringing my fingers, read another man's letter. Sidorov, the miserable killer, tore the pink wool of my imagination to shreds and pulled me into the corridors of his clear-headed madness. The letter began on the second page—I didn't dare look for the first:

> ...*lung's shot through and I'm a little cracked or, as Sergei says, flew off my nut. You don't just step off that nut, you fly. At any rate, jokes aside and tail out of the way... Let's get down to business, my friend Victoria...*
>
> *I did a three-month stint with the Makhno campaign—tiresome swindling, that's all... Only Volin's still back there.[1] Volin struts around in apostolic vestments and aims to become the Lenin of anarchism. Awful. And old man Makhno listens to him, strokes the dusty wires of his curls and lets the long snake of his peasant grin slip through his rotten teeth. And now I don't know*

*if there isn't a weed seed of anarchy in all this, and if we won't be wiping your lucky noses, you self-proclaimed Tsekists from your self-proclaimed Tsek, "made in Kharkov", your self-proclaimed capital.*[2] *Your good old boys don't like to recall the sins of their anarchist youth nowadays and laugh at them from the heights of statesmanship—to hell with them…*

*And then I got to Moscow. How did I get to Moscow? The boys were stepping on someone's toes in terms of requisition and otherwise. And I, ditherer that I am, stuck up for him. They really gave it to me—and rightly so. The wound was a trifle, but in Moscow, oh, Victoria, in Moscow I was struck dumb with misery. Every day the hospital nurses brought me grain porridge. Bridled with awe, they hauled it in on a big tray, and I grew to hate this urgent porridge, these above-plan supplies and this planned Moscow. Then I came across a handful of anarchists in the soviet. Show-offs and half-crazed old men, the whole lot of them. Poked my nose in at the Kremlin with a plan for real work. They patted me on the head and promised to make me a deputy, if only I'd mend my ways. I didn't mend my ways. What came next? Next came the front, the Cavalry and the soldiery, reeking of damp human blood and corpses.*

*Save me, Victoria. Statesmanship is driving me crazy, and I'm cockeyed with boredom. If you don't help—I'll up and die without any plan. And who'd want a soldier boy to up and die in so disorganized a way—certainly not you, Victoria, a bride who'll never be a wife. Here's sentimentality for you, the devil take it…*

*Now let's talk business. I'm bored in the army. I can't ride on account of the wound, and that means I can't fight. Using your influence, Victoria—let them send me to Italy. I'm learning the language and I'll be speaking in two months' time. The land's smouldering in Italy. Much of the work is done. All it needs is a couple of shots. I'll take one of them. Their king should be sent up to his forefathers. This is very important. That king of theirs is a nice old fellow, plays to the crowd and has pictures taken with tame socialists for the family journals.*

*But don't you mention shots or kings at the Tseka or the Commissariat for Foreign Affairs. They'll pat you on the head and mumble, "A romantic." Just tell them that he's sick, angry, drunk with despair, he wants the Italian sun and bananas. I've earned it, after all—or maybe I haven't? Just to get cured—and basta. And if not—let them send me to the Odessa Cheka… It's a very sensible outfit and…*

*How foolish, how wrong and foolish it is of me to write you this, my friend Victoria…*

*Italy has entered my heart like an obsession. The thought of that country, which I've never seen, is as sweet to me as a woman's name, as your name, Victoria…*

I read through the letter and lay down in my sagging, unclean bed, but sleep wouldn't come. Behind the wall a pregnant Jewess was crying in earnest; her lanky husband replied with a groaning murmur. They were recalling their looted possessions and blaming each other for ill luck. Then, sometime before dawn, Sidorov returned. The burnt-out candle was gasping for breath on the table. Sidorov took another candle-end out of his boot and, with unusual thoughtfulness, pressed it down onto the guttering wick. Our room was dark, gloomy, everything in it breathed with the damp stench of night, and only the window, filled with the moon's fire, shone like deliverance.

He came in and hid the letter, my wearisome neighbour. He sat down at the table, stooping, and opened the album of the city of Rome. The magnificent gilt-edged books stood before his expressionless olive face. Over his round back glimmered the jagged ruins of the Capitoline and the arena of the Circus, lit up by sunset. A photo of the royal family had been inserted there, between the large glossy pages. A scrap of paper torn from a calendar bore the image of friendly, feeble King Victor Emmanuel and his dark-haired wife, with Crown Prince Umberto and a whole brood of princesses.

…And so it's night, full of distant and painful chimes, a square of light in the damp darkness—and in this square, Sidorov's deathly face, a lifeless mask hovering over a candle's yellow flame.

# GEDALI

O N SABBATH EVES I am tormented by the rich sorrow of memories. Long ago, on these evenings, my grandfather would stroke the volumes of Ibn Ezra with his yellow beard. The old woman, in a lace headdress, would conjure with her gnarled fingers over the Sabbath candle and sob sweetly. On these evenings my child's heart would sway like a boat on enchanted waves... O the Talmuds of my childhood, reduced to dust! O the rich sorrow of memories!

I roam Zhitomir and search for the shy star. By the ancient synagogue, by her yellow and indifferent walls, old Jews are selling chalk, bluing, wicks—Jews with the beards of prophets, with passionate rags on their sunken chests...

Here before me is the bazaar and the death of the bazaar. The fat soul of abundance is killed. Mute padlocks hang on the stalls and the granite pavement is as clean as a dead man's bald pate. It twinkles and fades, the shy star...

Success came to me later, came just before sunset. Gedali's shop was tucked away among closely packed rows of stalls. Dickens, where was your shade that evening? In that old curiosity shop you'd have seen gilt shoes and ships' ropes, an antique compass and a stuffed eagle, a

Winchester hunting rifle engraved with the date 1810, and a broken stewpan.

Old Gedali paces around his treasures in the pink emptiness of the evening—a little shop-owner in smoky glasses and a green frock coat reaching down to the ground. He rubs his little white hands, tugs at his little grey beard and, bowing his head, heeds the invisible voices drifting down to him.

This shop is like the box of an inquisitive and serious boy who'll someday become a professor of botany. The shop has both buttons and a dead butterfly, and its little owner is named Gedali. Everyone's left the bazaar, but Gedali remains. He wends his way through a labyrinth of globes, skulls and dead flowers, whisks his motley brush of rooster feathers and blows the dust off the perished flowers.

We are sitting on empty beer kegs. Gedali twists and untwists his narrow beard. His top hat sways above us like a black turret. Warm air floats past us. The sky changes colour. Up there, high up, delicate blood flows from an overturned bottle, and I am enveloped in the faint odour of decay.

"The revolution—we'll say 'yes' to her, but will we say 'no' to the Sabbath?" so begins Gedali, entwining me in the silk straps of his smoky eyes. "'Yes,' I cry to the revolution, 'yes,' I cry to her, but she hides from Gedali, and all she sends our way is shooting..."

"The sun doesn't enter eyes that are closed," I answer the old man, "but we will rip those closed eyes open..."

"The Pole closed my eyes," the old man whispers, almost inaudibly. "The Pole is a mad dog. He takes a Jew and pulls out his beard—eh, that cur! And now they're beating him good, the mad dog. That's wonderful, that's the revolution! And then the one who beat the Pole says to me, 'We have to take your gramophone in account, Gedali…' 'But I love music, Pani,' I tell the revolution. 'You don't know what you like, Gedali—I'll shoot at you and then you'll find out, and I can't help shooting, because I'm the revolution…'"

"She can't help shooting, Gedali," I say to the old man, "because she's the revolution…"

"But the Pole shot, my dear Pan, because he's the counter-revolution. You shoot because you're the revolution. But the revolution is happiness. And happiness doesn't like orphans in the house. Good deeds are done by good men. The revolution is the good deed of good men. But good men do not kill. So the revolution is the work of bad men. But the Poles, too, are bad men. So who will tell Gedali where's the revolution and where's the counter-revolution? I once studied the Talmud—I love the commentaries of Rashi, the books of Maimonides. And there are other men of wisdom in Zhitomir. And here we are, all learned men, falling on our faces and crying out loud, 'Woe unto us, where is the sweet revolution?…'"

The old man fell silent. And we saw the first star cutting its path along the Milky Way.

"The Sabbath is coming," Gedali pronounced with significance. "Jews must go to the synagogue… Pan Comrade," he said, rising up, the top hat swaying like a black turret on his head, "bring a few good people to Zhitomir. Oh, what a shortage we have in our town. Oh, what a shortage! Bring good people, and we'll give them all our gramophones. We aren't ignorant. The International… We know what the International is. And I want an International of good people—I want them to take every soul into account and give it a first-grade ration. Here, soul, eat, go ahead, get some happiness out of life. It's you, Pan Comrade—it's you who doesn't know what they eat the International with…"

"They eat it with gunpowder," I answered the old man, "and season it with the best blood…"

And so she ascended her throne out of the deep-blue darkness, the young Sabbath.

"Gedali," I say, "today is Friday, and the evening is here. Where can I get a Jewish shortcake, a Jewish glass of tea, with some of that retired God in the glass?…"

"No place," Gedali answers, hanging a padlock on his box. "No place. There's a cook-shop next door, and good people did trade there, but nobody eats there nowadays, they weep…"

He fastened his green frock coat on three bone buttons. He dusted himself off with the rooster feathers, splashed a little water on his soft palms and walked off—tiny, lonely, dreamy, with a black top hat on his head and a big prayer book under his arm.

The Sabbath is coming. Gedali—the founder of a hopeless International—has gone off to the synagogue to pray.

# MY FIRST GOOSE

S AVITSKY, the Sixth Division commander, rose when he saw me, and I marvelled at the beauty of his gigantic body.[1] He rose and—with the purple of his breeches, with his crimson cap tilted to one side, with the decorations hammered into his chest—cut the hut in half, as a banner cuts the sky. He smelt of perfume and the overwhelmingly sweet coolness of soap. His long legs looked like a pair of girls clad in shiny shoulder-length jackboots.

He smiled at me, slapped his whip against the table and reached for the order that the chief of staff had just dictated. It was an order for Ivan Chesnokov to advance in the direction of Chugunov-Dobryvodka with the regiment entrusted to him and, upon coming into contact with the enemy, to destroy the same…

"…*For said destruction,*" wrote the division commander, filling the whole sheet with his scrawl, "*I hold Chesnokov entirely responsible, under pain of capital punishment, and I'll shoot him down on the spot, which you, Comrade Chesnokov, have no reason to doubt, as this isn't our first month working together at the front…*"

The Sixth Division commander signed the order with a flourish, tossed it to his orderlies and turned his face towards me. His grey eyes were dancing with joy.

"Report!" he shouted, and cleaved the air with his whip. Then he read the paper assigning me to the division staff.

"Make it an order!" said the division commander. "Make it an order and issue him a soldier's provisions—but he'll take care of his own privates. Can you read and write?"

"I can," I said, envying the iron and flowers of his youth. "I'm a graduate in law of Petersburg University…"

"You're one of those pansies!" he shouted, laughing. "And with glasses on your nose. What a little louse!… They send you without so much as checking with us—and you get cut to pieces for glasses around here. Think you'll get along, do you?"

"I'll get along," I said, and went off to the village with the quartermaster to find lodging for the night. The quartermaster carried my little trunk on his shoulders. The village street lay before us. The dying sun, yellow and round as a pumpkin, was breathing its last rosy breath into the sky.

We came up to a hut with painted carvings of garlands around the windows. The quartermaster suddenly stopped and said with an apologetic grin:

"We've got trouble with glasses around here, and you can't do a thing about it. A man of the highest distinction—he's a goner for sure. But you ruin a lady, the nicest little lady, and our fighting boys treat you real kind…"

He hesitated a moment with my little trunk on his shoulders, came right up to me, then jumped back in despair and ran into the first courtyard. Cossacks were sitting on hay in there, shaving one another.

"All right, men," said the quartermaster, placing my little trunk on the ground. "According to Comrade Savitsky's orders, you have to take this fellow into your billet, and no nonsense, on account of his having suffered on the fields of learning…"

The quartermaster reddened and walked away without looking back. I raised my hand to my cap and saluted the Cossacks. A young lad with lank, flaxen hair and a handsome Ryazan face walked up to my little trunk and flung it over the gate. Then he turned his backside towards me and, with unusual skill, began emitting shameful sounds.

"Artillery, zero calibre!" an older Cossack shouted and laughed. "Rapid fire…"

The lad exhausted his simple art and walked off. Then, crawling along the ground, I began gathering up the manuscripts and tattered old clothes that had fallen out of my little trunk. I gathered them up and carried them to the far end of the yard. Pork was cooking in a kettle that stood on bricks near the hut. It sent up a column of smoke, like one's family home in the village seen from a distance, mingling inside me a feeling of hunger and unprecedented loneliness. I covered my battered little trunk with hay, made a pillow out of it and lay down on the ground to read Lenin's speech at the Second Congress of the Comintern in *Pravda*. The sun fell on me from behind jagged hillocks, Cossacks stepped on my legs and the lad made fun of me relentlessly; Lenin's beloved lines travelled down a thorny path and couldn't reach me. So I put the paper aside and went over to the landlady, who was spinning yarn on the porch.

"Hostess," I said, "I gotta eat…"

The old woman lifted the flooded whites of her purblind eyes towards me and lowered them again.

"Comrade," she said, after a pause, "this business makes me want to hang myself."

"Mother of fucking Christ," I muttered angrily, and pushed the old woman in the chest with my fist. "I didn't come here to reason with you…"

Turning around, I saw someone else's sabre lying close by. A dour goose was wandering around the yard, calmly preening its feathers. I caught up with him, bent him to the ground. The goose's head cracked under my boot, cracked and bled. The white neck lay stretched out in the dung and the wings folded over the dead bird.

"Mother of fucking Christ!" I said, digging the sabre into the goose. "Roast it up for me, hostess."

The old woman, her blindness and glasses glinting, picked up the bird, wrapped it in her apron and carried it off to the kitchen.

"Comrade," she said, after a pause, "I want to hang myself," and shut the door behind her.

In the yard the Cossacks were already sitting around their kettle. They were motionless, straight-backed as priests. They hadn't looked at the goose.

"Our kind of lad," one of them said, winked, and scooped up some cabbage soup with his spoon.

The Cossacks commenced their dinner with the restrained elegance of peasants who hold one another in respect. I wiped the sabre down with sand, went out of the gate and came back in again, languishing. The moon hung over the yard like a cheap earring.

"Little brother," the eldest of the Cossacks, Surovkov, suddenly said to me, "come and have a bite with us till your goose is ready…"

He drew a spare spoon from his boot and handed it to me. We supped up the home-made cabbage soup and ate the pork.

"What're they writing in the newspaper?" asked the lad with the flaxen hair, making room for me.

"In the newspaper Lenin writes…" I said, pulling out *Pravda*. "Lenin writes we have a shortage in everything."

And loudly, like a deaf man triumphant, I read Lenin's speech to the Cossacks.

Evening enveloped me in the bracing dampness of its twilight sheets—evening laid its motherly palms on my blazing forehead. I read and rejoiced, and caught, rejoicing, the mysterious curve of Lenin's straight line.

"Truth tickles every nostril," Surovkov said when I'd finished. "Question is, how do you pull it out of the pile? But Lenin hits it straight away, like a hen pecking at a grain."

That's what Surovkov, platoon commander of the staff squadron, said about Lenin, and then we went to sleep in the hayloft. There were six of us, huddling together for warmth, our legs tangled, under a roof full of holes that let in the stars. I had dreams—dreamt of women—and only my heart, crimson with murder, creaked and bled.

# THE REBBE

"... $\mathbf{A}$LL THINGS ARE MORTAL. Only a mother is destined for eternal life. And when a mother is no longer among the living, she leaves behind a memory that no one dares to desecrate. A mother's memory nourishes compassion within us, just as the ocean, the boundless ocean, nourishes the rivers that cleave the universe…"

These were Gedali's words. He pronounced them with significance. The dying evening surrounded him with the rosy haze of its sadness. The old man said:

"The doors and windows have been knocked out of Hasidism's passionate edifice, but it is immortal, like a mother's soul… Its eyes have been gouged from their sockets, but Hasidism still stands at the crossroads of the furious winds of history."

So said Gedali, and, having finished his prayers at the synagogue, he led me to Rebbe Motale, the last rebbe of the Chernobyl dynasty.

Gedali and I went up the main street. White churches glittered in the distance like fields of buckwheat. A cannon wheel groaned around the corner. Two pregnant Ukrainian girls walked out of a gate, their necklaces jangling, and sat on a bench. The shy star lit up amid the orange battle scenes of sunset, and peace, a Sabbath peace, descended on the crooked roofs of the Zhitomir ghetto.

"Here," Gedali whispered, pointing to a long house with a broken pediment.

We entered a room that was stony and barren, like a morgue. Rebbe Motale sat at the table, surrounded by liars and the bedevilled. He wore a sable cap and a white gown bound with a rope. The rebbe sat with his eyes closed and his thin fingers fumbling in the yellow down of his beard.

"Where has the Jew come from?" he asked, lifting his eyelids.

"From Odessa," I answered.

"A pious city," said the rebbe, "the star of our exile, the involuntary well of our calamities!… What is the Jew's occupation?"

"I am putting the adventures of Hershel of Ostropol[1] into verse."

"A great task," whispered the rebbe, lowering his eyelids. "The jackal whines when he is hungry, any fool is fool enough for despondency, and only the wise man rends the veil of being with laughter… What has the Jew studied?"

"The Bible."

"What does the Jew seek?"

"Joy."

"Reb Mordkhe," said the *tsaddik*,[2] shaking his beard, "let the young man take a seat at the table, let him eat this Sabbath eve with other Jews, let him rejoice that he is alive and not dead, let him clap his hands when his neighbours dance, let him drink wine if he is given wine…"

And Reb Mordkhe scurried over to me—a timeworn jester with turned-out eyelids, a tiny hunchbacked old man, no taller than a ten-year-old boy.

"Oh, my dear and so young a man!" said the ragged Reb Mordkhe, winking at me. "Oh, how many wealthy fools I have known in Odessa, how many poor wise men I have known in Odessa! Sit down at the table, young man, and drink the wine you won't be given…"

We all sat together—the bedevilled, the liars, the loafers. In the corner, moaning over their prayer books, stood broad-shouldered Jews who looked like fishermen and apostles. Gedali dozed against the wall in his green frock coat, like a gay little bird. And suddenly I saw a young man seated behind him, a young man with the face of Spinoza, with Spinoza's mighty brow and a nun's sallow face. He was smoking and quivering, like a fugitive captured after a chase and brought back to prison. Ragged Mordkhe crept up behind him, snatched the cigarette from his mouth and ran back to me.

"That is the rebbe's son, Ilya," Mordkhe rasped, approaching me with the bleeding flesh of his mangled eyelids. "A damned son, the last son, a disobedient son…"

Mordkhe shook his fist at the young man and spat in his face.

"Blessed be the Lord," Rebbe Motale Bratslavsky's voice rang out, and he broke bread with his monkish fingers.

"Blessed be the God of Israel, who has chosen us among all the nations of the earth…"

The rebbe blessed the food and we sat down at table. Outside the window horses neighed and Cossacks shouted. The desert of war yawned outside the window. The rebbe's son smoked one cigarette after another amid the silence and prayers. When the supper was over, I was the first to rise.

"My dear and so young a man," Mordkhe muttered behind my back and pulled at my belt, "if there were no one in this world but evil rich men and poor tramps, how would holy men live?"

I gave the old man money and went out into the street. Gedali and I parted ways and I walked on to the station. There, at the station, on the agitprop train of the First Cavalry Army, I was awaited by the glare of countless lights, the magical glimmer of the wireless, the stubborn running of the printing press and an unfinished article for *The Red Cavalryman* newspaper.

## THE ROAD TO BRODY

I MOURN FOR THE BEES. They've been harried to death by warring armies. There are no more bees in Volyn.

We've defiled their indescribable hives. We've wiped them out with sulphur and blown them to shreds with gunpowder. Smouldering rags emitted their stench in the sacred republics of the bees. Perishing, they flew slowly, with a barely audible buzz. Deprived of bread, we extracted honey with our sabres. There are no more bees in Volyn.

The chronicle of mundane atrocities weighs on me relentlessly, like heart disease. Yesterday saw the first bloody battle at Brody. Wandering lost on the blue earth, we didn't even suspect it—neither I nor my friend Afonka Bida. The horses had got their grain in the morning. The rye was tall, the sun beautiful, and the soul, which didn't deserve these shining and fleeting skies, longed for leisurely pains. That's why I forced Afonka's unflinching lips to bend to my sorrows.

"All through the Cossack villages the womenfolk talk of the bee, how she's kind-hearted," began my friend, the platoon commander, "talk all kinds of things. Did people do wrong by Christ, or didn't they? The rest'll find that out in due time. But the womenfolk in the villages say here is Christ pining away on the Cross. And gnats of all kinds are flying up to Christ, so as to torture him. And he sets his eyes on them, and his spirits sink. But the countless gnats, they can't see his eyes. And a bee's flying around Christ, too.

"'Strike him,' the gnats shout at the bee. 'Strike him one for us…'

"'Can't do it,' says the bee, raising her wings over Christ. 'Can't do it—he's carpenter class…'

"You've got to understand the bee," concludes Afonka, my platoon commander. "Let the bee tough it out for a while. It's for her sake, too, that we're getting our hands dirty…"

Waving at the thought, Afonka struck up a song. It was a song about a light-bay stallion. Eight Cossacks—Afonka's platoon—joined in.

The light-bay stallion, Dzhigit by name, belonged to a Cossack captain who got himself drunk on the Day of the Beheading. So sang Afonka, drawing his voice out like a string and dozing off. Dzhigit was a loyal steed, but on feast days the captain's desires knew no bounds. There were five jugs of vodka on the Day of the Beheading. After the fourth, the captain mounted his steed and rode off for heaven. The climb was a long one, but Dzhigit was a loyal steed. They arrived in heaven, and the captain grabbed for the fifth jug. But they'd left it on earth—that last jug. Then the captain broke down and wept at the futility of his efforts. He wept, and Dzhigit flicked his ears, staring at his master…

So sang Afonka, clinking and dozing off. The song wafted like smoke. And we were riding towards the heroic sunset.

Its boiling rivers ran down the embroidered towels of peasant fields. A rosy silence. The land lay like a cat's back, overgrown with the shimmering fur of grains. Up on a hill crouched the little mud-brick village of Klekotów. The sight of deathly, jagged Brody awaited us over the pass. But at Klekotów a shot burst loudly in our faces. Two Polish soldiers glanced at us from behind a hut. Their horses were tied to stakes. The enemy's light battery came riding briskly up the hill. Bullets stretched in strings along the road.

"Move out!" Afonka said.

And we fled.

O Brody! The mummies of your trampled passions had breathed their insurmountable poison upon me. I already felt the deadly chill of eye sockets brimming with cooling tears. And now—a staggering gallop carries me away from the chipped stone of your synagogues…

*Brody, August 1920*

# THE TACHANKA DOCTRINE

T HEY SENT ME A COACHMAN from headquarters, or a wagoner, as we call them around here. Grishchuk is his name. He's thirty-nine years old. His story is awful.

He spent five years as a German prisoner of war, ran off a few months ago, tramped through Lithuania and north-west Russia, reached Volyn, and then he was caught in Belyov by the most brainless mobilization committee in the world, which assigned him to active duty. Grishchuk had only fifty *verst*s to go before he reached the Kremenets District, the land of his birth. He has a wife and kids in the Kremenets District. He hasn't been home in five years and two months. The mobilization committee made him my wagoner, and I've ceased to be a pariah among the Cossacks.

I am the proud owner of a *tachanka*[1] and of the coachman that goes with it. *Tachanka!* This word has come to serve as the base of the triangle on which our way of life rests: slash—*tachanka*—steed…

Through the caprice of our civil strife, the garden-variety *britchka*,[2] conveyance of priests and assessors, has got its chance: it has become a formidable and agile combat vehicle, has created a new strategy and new tactics, has distorted the familiar face of war and has brought forth heroes and geniuses of the *tachanka*. Makhno, whom we've stifled, was one of them. Makhno, who made the *tachanka* the axis of his mysterious and cunning strategy, abolished the infantry, the artillery, even the cavalry, and replaced those hulking masses with three hundred machine guns screwed onto *britchkas*. Makhno, as Protean as nature itself. Hay carts, lined up in battle formation, seize towns. A wedding procession approaches the local district's executive committee, opens concentrated fire, and a puny little priest, brandishing the black flag of anarchy over his head, demands that the authorities hand over the bourgeoisie, hand over the proletariat, the wine, the music.

An army of *tachankas* is capable of unprecedented manoeuvrability.

Budyonny demonstrated this just as well as Makhno. It's hard to cut such an army down, and capture is unthinkable. The machine gun buried under a hayrick, the *tachanka* drawn off into a peasant's threshing barn—they cease to be military units. These hidden emplacements, these implied but intangible items, add to up to the Ukrainian village of recent days—fierce, rebellious and self-interested. Makhno can whip such an army, with its ammunition scattered all over, into fighting condition in an hour; he needs even less time to demobilize it.

Here, in Budyonny's regular cavalry, the *tachanka* doesn't hold such exclusive sway. Nevertheless, all our machine-gun detachments ride around on *britchkas*. The imaginative

Cossack distinguishes between two types of *tachanka*: the colonists' and the assessors'. But this is no mere imagining—it's a real distinction.

In the assessors' *britchka*s, in these rickety wagons fashioned without love or ingenuity, wretched, red-nosed bureaucrats— a sleep-deprived bunch rushing off to post-mortems and criminal inquiries—would rattle across the wheat steppes of the Kuban. The colonists' *britchka*s, meanwhile, came to us from Samara and the Urals, the fertile tracts of the German colonies along the Volga. The spacious oaken backs of the colonists' *tachanka*s are covered with homey artwork—plump garlands of pink German flowers. Their sturdy bottoms are bound in iron. Their mechanisms rest on unforgettable springs. I feel the ardour of many generations in these springs, which now beat along the upturned highways of Volyn.

I experience the rapture of the first-time owner. Every day after lunch we harness up. Grishchuk leads the horses from the stable. They're improving by the day. With proud joy I note the matt sheen on their groomed flanks. We rub down the horses' swollen legs, trim their manes, throw the Cossack harness—a tangled, shrivelled network of thin straps—over their backs and leave the yard at a trot. Grishchuk sits sideways on the box; my seat is padded with floral sackcloth and hay that smells of perfume and serenity. The tall wheels creak in the granular white sand. Patches of blooming poppy colour the land and ruined churches gleam in the hillocks. High above the road, in a niche smashed by a shell, stands a brown statue of St Ursula with bare, round hands. Thin ancient letters weave an uneven chain on the blackened gilt of the pediment… "For the glory of Jesus and His Holy Mother…"

Lifeless Jewish shtetls cling to the feet of lordly estates. Prophetic peacocks shimmer on brick fences—dispassionate apparitions in the blue expanse. Hidden behind sprawling shanties, a synagogue squats on the barren soil—eyeless, gap-toothed, as round as a Hasidic hat. Narrow-shouldered Jews hang about glumly at the crossroads. And the image of southern Jews flares up in my memory—jovial, pot-bellied, bubbling like cheap wine. They have nothing in common with the bitter arrogance of these long bony backs, these tragic yellow beards. There is no fat, no warm pulse of blood in these passionate, painfully etched features. The movements of the Galician and Volynian Jew are violent, jerky and offensive to good taste, but the power of their grief is full of gloomy grandeur and their secret contempt for the Pan knows no limits. Watching them, I understood the whole burning history of this faraway region, tales of Talmudists who rented out taverns, of rabbis who engaged in usury, of girls who were raped by Polish soldiers and on whose account Polish magnates fought duels.

# THE DEATH OF DOLGUSHOV

T HE CURTAINS OF BATTLE advanced towards the town. At noon Korochayev flew past us in a black felt cloak. The disgraced Fourth Division commander fought alone, seeking death. Galloping by, he shouted:

"Communications cut—Radzivilov and Brody in flames!…"

And off he went—all black and fluttering, with pupils of coal.

The brigades were regrouping on the board-flat plain. The sun rolled in the purple dust. Wounded men were eating in the ditches. Nurses lay on the grass, singing softly. Afonka's scouts combed the field, searching for corpses and uniforms. Afonka rode by within two paces of me and said, without turning his head:

"They whipped us good. Sure as hell. Got a notion about the division commander—getting canned. Fighters have doubts…"

The Poles reached the woods, about three *verst*s from us, and positioned machine guns somewhere close by. The bullets whine and squeal. Their lament grows unbearably loud. The bullets shoot the earth, digging into it, trembling with impatience. Vytyagaychenko, the regimental commander, who'd been snoring in the blazing sun, cried out in his sleep and woke up. He mounted his horse and rode over to the lead squadron. His face was creased, streaked red from uncomfortable sleep, and his pockets were full of plums.

"Son of a bitch," he said angrily and spat out a plum stone. "A damned waste of time. Timoshka, throw up the flag!"

"So we're going?" Timoshka asked, taking the pole from his stirrups and unwinding the banner, which bore a painted star and some writing about the Third International.

"We'll see when we get there," Vytyagaychenko said, and suddenly shouted wildly: "Girls, hop on them horses! Call your men, squadron commanders!…"

Buglers sounded the alarm. The squadrons formed a column. A wounded man climbed out of a ditch and, shading his eyes with his palm, said to Vytyagaychenko:

"Taras Grigoryevich, they made me delegate down there. Looks, you know, like you're leaving us behind…"

"You'll fight 'em off," Vytyagaychenko muttered and made his horse rear.

"We've got this idea, Taras Grigoryevich, that we won't manage to fight 'em off," the wounded man called after him.

"Quit your moaning," Vytyagaychenko said, turning back. "Don't worry, I won't leave you." Then he gave the order to move off.

And suddenly the wailing woman's voice of Afonka Bida, my friend, rang out:

"Don't start us out at a trot, Taras Grigoryevich—we've got five *verst*s to cover. How're we supposed to hack 'em down on worn-out horses… No point in rushing—we'll pick our fruits when the time comes…"

"At a walk!" Vytyagaychenko commanded, without looking up.

The regiment rode off.

"If my notion 'bout the division commander's right," Afonka whispered, hanging back, "if he's getting canned, then soap the withers and knock out the props. Period."

Tears streamed from his eyes. I stared at Afonka in amazement. He spun around like a top, clutched his cap, snorted, whooped and dashed off.

Grishchuk with his silly *tachanka* and I—we stayed back alone, knocking about until evening between walls of fire. The division staff vanished. Other units wouldn't take us in. The Poles entered Brody and were dislodged by a counterattack. We rode up to the town cemetery. Polish patrolmen sprang out from behind the graves, shouldered their rifles and opened fire on us. Grishchuk turned around. His *tachanka* yowled with all four of its wheels.

"Grishchuk!" I cried through the whining and the wind.

"A joke," he replied sadly.

"We're done for," I cried out, seized by the rapture of ruin. "Done for, old man!"

"Why do womenfolk take the trouble?" he said even more sadly. "Why all the matchmaking, marrying, all the kinfolk dancing at weddings…"

A rosy trail lit up in the sky and died out. The Milky Way showed through the stars.

"It's a laugh," Grishchuk said sorrowfully and pointed his whip at a man sitting by the roadside. "A laugh, womenfolk taking the trouble…"

The man sitting by the roadside was Dolgushov, the telephonist. He looked straight at us, his legs thrown wide apart.

"Listen," said Dolgushov when we rode up to him. "I'm finished… Got it?"

"Got it," Grishchuk replied, stopping the horses.

"Got to waste a cartridge on me," Dolgushov said sternly.

He sat leaning against a tree. His boots were stuck wide apart. Without taking his eyes off me he carefully lifted his shirt. His stomach had been torn out, his guts were sliding onto his knees, and you could see his heartbeats.

"The Poles'll come, have some fun with me. Take my papers, write my mother what's what…"

"No," I said, and spurred my horse.

Dolgushov spread his blue palms out on the ground and examined them incredulously.

"Running away?" he murmured, sliding down. "Run, you bastard…"

Sweat slid over my body. The machine guns were hammering faster and faster, with hysterical obstinacy. Afonka Bida came galloping towards us, encircled by the halo of sunset.

"We're pelting 'em good," he shouted cheerfully. "What've you got going here?"

I pointed him to Dolgushov and rode off to the side.

They spoke briefly—I didn't hear the words. Dolgushov handed the platoon commander his booklet. Afonka stuffed it into his boot and shot Dolgushov in the mouth.

"Afonya," I said with a pitiful smile, riding up to the Cossack, "I just couldn't myself."

"Get away," he said, turning pale, "or you're dead! You care for our kind, four-eyes, like a cat cares for a mouse…"

And he cocked his rifle.

I rode off at a walk, without turning, sensing cold and death on my back.

"Hey!" Grishchuk shouted behind me. "Quit fooling around!" He grabbed Afonka by the arm.

"Lackey bastard!" Afonka cried. "He won't get away from me…"

Grishchuk caught up with me at the turn. Afonka was gone. He'd ridden off in the other direction.

"You see, Grishchuk," I said. "Today I lost Afonka, my first friend…"

Grishchuk took a wrinkled apple out from his driver's seat.

"Eat," he said to me. "Eat, please…"

And I accepted Grishchuk's charity and ate his apple with sadness and reverence.

*Brody, August 1920*

## THE SECOND
## BRIGADE COMMANDER

B UDYONNY STOOD by a tree in red trousers with silver stripes. The Second Brigade commander had just been killed. The Army commander appointed Kolesnikov to replace him.

An hour ago Kolesnikov had been a regimental commander. A week ago Kolesnikov had been a squadron commander.

The new brigadier had been summoned to see Budyonny. The Army commander was waiting, standing by a tree. Kolesnikov rode up with Almazov, his commissar.

"Bastards are closing in," the Army commander declared with that dazzling smile of his. "It's win or croak. No other way. Got that?"

"Got it," Kolesnikov replied, his eyes bulging.

"You run—I have you shot," the Army commander said, smiled and turned his eyes towards the chief of the Special Section.

"Yes, sir," said the Special Section chief.

"Roll on, Koleso!"[1] some Cossack standing off to the side shouted cheerfully.

Budyonny turned swiftly on his heels and saluted the new brigade commander. The latter stuck five red, youthful fingers to the peak of his cap, broke out in a sweat and went off along a ploughed boundary path. The horses were waiting for him about a hundred *sazhens*[2] off. He walked with his head down, shifting his long crooked legs with agonizing slowness. The blaze of sunset was spreading above him, crimson and implausible, like impending death.

And suddenly, on the outstretched earth, on the turned-up, yellow nakedness of the fields, we saw nothing but Kolesnikov's narrow back, with dangling arms and drooping head in a grey cap.

An orderly brought him a horse.

He jumped into the saddle and galloped off to his brigade without looking back. The squadrons were waiting for him near the big road, the highway to Brody.

A groaning "hurrah", rent by the wind, finally reached us.

Training my field glasses on the brigade commander, I saw him circling on his horse amid pillars of blue dust.

"Kolesnikov is leading the brigade," said an observer positioned in a tree above our heads.

"Very good," Budyonny replied, lit a cigarette and closed his eyes.

The "hurrah" fell silent. The cannonade broke off. Unnecessary shrapnel burst above the woods. And we heard the great silence of hacking.

"Hearty little fellow," said the Army commander, rising up. "Looking for glory. Believe he'll pull it off."

Calling for horses, Budyonny rode off to the battlefield. The staff followed him.

I happened to see Kolesnikov that same evening, an hour after the Poles were destroyed. He was riding in front of his brigade, alone, on a light-dun stallion, and dozing. His right arm hung in a sling. A Cossack cavalryman carried an unfurled banner ten paces behind him. The head squadron lazily led the others in singing bawdy verses. The brigade trailed along, dusty and endless, like peasant carts heading to a fair. Weary brass bands panted at the rear.

That evening, in Kolesnikov's manner of riding, I saw a Tatar khan's lordly indifference and recognized the battle training of the celebrated Kniga,[3] the wilful Pavlichenko and the captivating Savitsky.

*Brody, August 1920*

# SASHKA THE CHRIST

S ASHKA—that was his name. They nicknamed him Christ
on account of his meekness. He was a community shepherd in the Cossack village and hadn't done any hard work
since the age of fourteen, when he'd caught a foul disease.
This is how it all came about:

Tarakanych, Sashka's stepfather, went off to the city of
Grozny for the winter and joined up with a peasant collective
there. It turned out to be a successful collective, made up
of sturdy Ryazan men. Tarakanych handled the carpentry
for them and was making a nice profit. He couldn't keep up
with the orders and had the boy sent up as an apprentice; the
village could get along without Sashka in the winter. Sashka
put in a week with his stepfather. Then came Saturday. They
laid aside their tools and sat down to tea. It was October,
but the air was mild. They opened the window and heated
up their second samovar. A beggar woman was going from
window to window. She knocked on their sill and said:

"Good day, visiting peasants. Consider my situation."

"What d'you mean, situation?" Tarakanych said. "Come
on in, cripple."

The beggar woman fumbled behind the wall, then hopped

into the room. She walked up to the table and bowed from the waist. Tarakanych snatched her kerchief, threw it aside and ran his fingers through her hair. The beggar woman's hair was dull, hoary, all wispy and dusty.

"Goodness, what a fine, rowdy fellow!" she said. "It's a real circus with you, ain't it? Don't be squeamish just 'cause I'm old," she whispered quickly and clambered up onto the bench. Tarakanych lay down with her and got as much pleasure out of her as he could. The beggar woman kept tossing back her head and laughing.

"It's finally raining on the old woman," she laughed. "I'll sprout two hundred *pood*s to the *desyatina*..."[1]

After she said this, she spotted Sashka, who was drinking tea at the table and wouldn't lift his eyes to God's world.

"Your boy?" she asked Tarakanych.

"Sort of," said Tarakanych. "The wife's."

"There's a good boy, his eyes are popping," said the woman. "Well, get over here, then."

Sashka went over to her—and caught a foul disease. But no one thought of foul diseases just then. Tarakanych gave the beggar woman the bones from their supper and a silver five-copeck piece, bright and shiny.

"Rub it clean with sand, God-fearing woman," said Tarakanych, "and it'll look even finer. Offer it to the Lord God on a dark night, and that fiver, it'll shine instead of the moon..."

The cripple wrapped herself up in her kerchief, took the bones and left. While two weeks later, things became clear for the men. They suffered plenty from the foul disease, tried to fight it all winter, treated themselves with herbs. In the spring they went back to the village, to their peasant work.

The village stood about nine *verst*s from the railroad. Tarakanych and Sashka walked through the fields. The earth lay in the April dampness. Emeralds glimmered in black ditches. Green shoots embroidered an intricate stitch in the earth. And the earth gave off a sour smell, like a soldier's wife at dawn. The first herd trickled down from the mounds, and foals played in the horizon's blue expanses.

Tarakanych and Sashka walked along paths that were barely noticeable.

"Tarakanych, let me go and be a shepherd for the community," said Sashka.

"What for?"

"I can't stand it—the shepherds have such a wonderful life."

"I won't permit it," Tarakanych said.

"For God's sake, let me go, Tarakanych," repeated Sashka. "All the saints came from shepherds."

"Sashka the saint," the stepfather broke out laughing, "went and caught syphilis from the Mother of God."

They walked by the bend at the Red Bridge, passed the grove, the pasture, and saw the cross on the village church. The women were still rooting around in their vegetable gardens, while the Cossacks were sitting among the lilacs, drinking vodka and singing. It was about half a *verst*'s walk to Tarakanych's hut.

"Pray God it'll all turn out," Tarakanych said and crossed himself.

They came up to the hut and looked in the little window. There was no one inside the hut. Sashka's mother was milking the cow in the stable. The men crept up to her in silence. Then Tarakanych laughed and cried out behind the woman's back:

"Motya, your highness, rustle up some supper for your guests…"

The woman turned, trembled, then ran out of the stable and began circling about the yard. Then she returned to her place and threw herself on Tarakanych's chest, quivering.

"What a fool you are, a homely fool," said Tarakanych and gently pushed her away. "Show me the children…"

"The children have left our yard," said the woman, all white, then ran through the yard again and fell to the ground. "Oh, Alyoshenka," she cried out wildly, "our kids have left us, feet first…"

Tarakanych waved his hand at her and went over to the neighbours. The neighbours told him that God had taken his boy and girl last week, with typhus. Motya had written to him, but he'd probably set out before getting the letter. Tarakanych returned to the hut. His woman was kindling the stove.

"You sure got rid of 'em, Motya, free and clear," said Tarakanych. "Ought to rip you apart."

He sat down at the table and began to grieve—and grieved till bedtime, ate meat and drank vodka, and didn't go about his chores. He snored at the table, woke up and snored again.

Motya laid out the bed for herself and her husband, and for Sashka on the side. She blew out the lamp and lay down with her husband. Sashka tossed and turned on the hay in his corner, with his eyes open. He didn't sleep and saw, as in a dream, the hut, a star in the window, the edge of the table and the horse collars under his mother's bed. A forceful vision conquered him; he succumbed to his fantasies and rejoiced in his waking dream. It seemed to him that two silver cords descended from the sky, twisting into a thick thread, and that a cradle was attached to them—a cradle of rosewood covered with carvings. It rocked high above the earth and far from the sky, and the silver cords swayed and shimmered. Sashka lay in the cradle, and the air fanned him. The air, as loud as music, blew in from the fields, and a rainbow blossomed above the unripened grain.

Sashka rejoiced in his waking dream and kept shutting his eyes, so as not to see the horse collars under his mother's bed. Then he heard a quiet puffing coming from Motya's stove bench and it occurred to him that Tarakanych was tumbling his mother.

"Tarakanych," he said loudly. "I have some business with you."

"What business, in the middle of the night?" Tarakanych called back angrily. "Sleep, you little louse…"

"I swear on the Cross, I have some business with you," Sashka replied. "Come out into the yard."

And out in the yard, beneath the unfading star, Sashka said to his stepfather:

"Don't hurt mother, Tarakanych—you're tainted."

"Do you know my temper?" asked Tarakanych.

"I know your temper, but you see mother, what a body she has. Her legs are pure, and her breast is pure. Don't hurt her, Tarakanych. We're tainted."

"Kind fellow," the stepfather replied. "Step back from bloodshed, from my temper. Here, take twenty copecks, sleep it off, sober up…"

"I've got no use for twenty copecks," Sashka muttered. "Let me go be a shepherd for the community…"

"I won't permit that," said Tarakanych.

"Let me go and be a shepherd," Sashka muttered, "or I'll come clean with mother, what sort of men we are. Why should she suffer with such a body?…"

Tarakanych turned around, went into the barn and brought out an axe.

"Sashka the saint," he said in a whisper. "That's all there is to it… I'll chop you down, saint…"

"You won't chop me down for a woman," the boy said, almost inaudibly, and bowed down before his stepfather. "You pity me. Let me go and be a shepherd…"

"The hell with you," said Tarakanych and threw the axe aside. "Go be a shepherd."

And he returned to the hut and slept with his wife.

That same morning Sashka went to hire himself out to the Cossacks, and from that time on he lived as a community shepherd. He became known throughout the area for his simple-heartedness, the villagers nicknamed him "Sashka the

Christ", and he lived as a shepherd till the day he was called up for service. Old peasants, the very worst of them, would come out to the pasture to see him and to wag their tongues; women would run to Sashka to get some relief from their husbands' terrible ways, and they weren't cross with Sashka over his love and his disease. Sashka got called up in the first year of the war. He spent four years at the front and returned to the village when the Whites were riding roughshod over it. Sashka was goaded into leaving for the village of Platovskaya, where a detachment was being formed against the Whites. Semyon Mikhaylovich Budyonny, a former cavalry sergeant major, was running things in this detachment, along with three of his brothers: Yemelyan, Lukyan and Denis. Sashka went to Platovskaya, and there his fate was sealed. He was in Budyonny's regiment, in his brigade, division, and the First Cavalry Army. He went to rescue heroic Tsaritsyn, joined up with Voroshilov's Tenth Army,[2] fought at Voronezh, at Kastornaya and at General's Bridge on the Donets. Sashka entered the Polish campaign as a transport driver, because he'd been injured and was considered an invalid.

That's how it all came about. I've recently struck up an acquaintance with Sashka the Christ and shifted my little trunk to his cart. We've greeted the morning light and accompanied the setting sun quite often by now. And when the wilful desire of battle would bring us together—we'd sit in the evenings by glittering mounds of earth, or boil tea in a sooty kettle in the woods, or sleep side by side in freshly mown fields with hungry horses tethered to our legs.

# THE LIFE STORY OF
## PAVLICHENKO, MATVEI RODIONYCH

C OUNTRYMEN, COMRADES, BROTHERS! Heed, in the
name of all mankind, the life story of the Red General
Matvei Pavlichenko.[1] He was a herdsman, this general—
a herdsman on the estate of Lidino, which belonged to
Nikitinsky, and he herded the master's pigs till life doled him
out some stripes for his shoulder-straps, and so Matyushka
commenced herding cattle. And who knows? If he'd been
born in Australia, then our Matvei—the honourable
Rodionych—well, it's a sure thing, my friends, that he'd
have worked his way up to elephants, that our Matyushka
would've been herding elephants. But as much as it pains me
to say, we haven't got any elephants in this Stavropol province
of ours. In this sprawling Stavropol country of ours, I'll tell
you frankly, there isn't a single animal larger than a buffalo.
And what joy can a poor peasant get out of the buffalo? The
Russian man finds it dull tormenting the buffalo. Give us
orphans a horse to torment till doomsday, a horse—so that
her soul gives out on the boundary path along with her guts…

And so I'm herding this cattle of mine, cows on every
side. I'm shot through with milk, stink like a sliced udder,

and I've got bull calves walking around me for propriety's sake, mousy-grey bull calves. Pure freedom has fallen on the fields, the grass crunches for all the world to hear, the heavens unfurl above me like a multi-row accordion—and the heavens, boys, can be very blue in the province of Stavropol. And so I'm herding along like this, having nothing better to do than swap melodies with the wind on my fife, till one of the old fellows says to me:

"Matvei, go and see Nastya," he says.

"Why?" I say. "You having a laugh at me or what, old man?"

"Go and see her," he says. "She's asking."

And so I go.

"Nastya," I say, and blacken with all my blood. "Nastya," I say, "you having a laugh at me or what?"

But she doesn't say a word, just tears away from me and runs with all 'er might, and we're running together till we're in the pasture, and we stand there dead tired, red, out of breath.

"Matvei," Nastya says to me then, "it's three Sundays since the spring fishing season, when all the fisherman went to the shore—and you went with them, with your head down. Why was your head down, Matvei—have you got some thought gnawing at your heart? Answer me…"

And I tell her:

"Nastya," I tell her. "I've got nothing to tell you. My head's not a rifle—it's got no foresight, and no back-sight either. And you know my heart, Nastya—it's all empty, it must be shot through with milk. It's an awful thing, how I stink of milk…"

And Nastya, I see, is about to burst.

"I'll swear on the Cross," she bursts out, laughing her head off, laughing at the top of her lungs over the whole steppe, like she's banging a drum. "I'll swear on the cross, you've been winking at the ladies…"

So we talk nonsense for a while, and soon enough we get married. And so Nastya and I start living as best we can, and we sure could. We were hot all night, hot in the wintertime—went around naked all night long, tearing at each other's hides. We lived swell, like devils, up until the old man shows up a second time.

"Matvei," he says, "the master's been touching your wife all over the place lately, and he'll get 'er yet, the master…"

And I say:

"No," I say. "No, and excuse me, old man, or I'll mow you down right here on the spot."

The old man, of course, took off at full pelt, and that day I covered twenty *verst*s of land on my feet. I covered a large chunk of land on my feet that day, and in the evening I turned up at the estate of Lidino, at my merry master Nikitinsky's. He was sitting in the upstairs room, old as the hills, taking apart three saddles—one English, one dragoon, one Cossack—and I stood stock still by the door, like a burdock, stood stock still for a solid hour, and nothing came of it. But then he laid eyes on me.

"What do you want?" he says.

"I want to settle accounts."

"Have you got some intention?"

"Haven't got no intentions, but I want to settle."

Then he turned his eyes to the side, turned off the highway into a side road, laid his scarlet saddle cloths on the floor—redder than the tsar's flags, they were—and the old geezer stood on them and commenced fuming.

"Freedom to the freedman," he tells me, fuming. "I've tickled all your mothers, you Orthodox Christians. We can settle accounts—but Matyusha, my friend, don't you owe me a trifle?"

"Heh-heh," I answer him. "Now that's a good one, you joker—so help me God, you're a hell of a joker! It's you that owes me my wages…"

"Wages," my master grinds out through his choppers and throws me down on my knees, stamping his feet, and plugs my ears with the Father and Son and Holy Spirit. "Wages, you want—but my yoke you've forgotten, you! Last year you busted my ox-yoke—where is it, my yoke?"

"I'll give you your yoke," I say to my master, and I raise my foolish eyes to him, standing on my knees, lower than any lowland. "You'll have your yoke, but don't press me on the debts, old man—give me some time…"

And so, my boys of Stavropol, my countrymen and comrades, my brothers, the master waited on my debts for five years. I wasted away for five wasted years, until the year '18 came to visit me, a poor wastrel. He rode in on gay stallions—on those Kabardian horses of his. He came with a long train of troops, and all kinds of songs. And hell, what a darling you are, '18! Will we really never whoop it up again, blood of my blood, my darling '18? We sang up your songs, drank up your wine, established your truth, and all that's left of you is clerks. But hell, my darling! It wasn't the clerk flying about the Kuban in those days, sending generals' souls into the air at a step's distance. Matvei Rodionych lay covered in blood at Prikumsk back then, and there was only a day's march of five *verst*s between Matvei Rodionych and the estate of Lidino. And I rode out there alone, without a detachment, and when I went into the upstairs room, I went in quiet. The local authority's sitting there, in the upstairs room, and Nikitinsky's taking the tea round, bowing and scraping to 'em. When he sees me, though, he turns white as a sheet—but I take off my Kuban cap to him.

"Good day," I say to the people. "Good day, and my regards. Welcome your guest, master, or how will it be with us?"

"It will be peaceful and dignified," one of the men answers me, and I can tell he's a surveyor by the way he says it. "It will be peaceful and dignified, but you, Comrade Pavlichenko, have galloped a long way to see us, it seems. Mud crosses your face. We, the local authority, are terrified by such faces. Why is this so?"

"It's so," I answer. "It's so, you local and cold-blooded authority, because one of the cheeks in my face has been burning for five years—it burns when I'm in the trenches, burns when I'm with a woman, and it'll burn at the Last Judgement. At the Last Judgement," I say, and look at Nikitinsky, all cheerful-like, but he's got no eyes left—just two balls in the middle of his face, as if they'd rolled those balls into position under his forehead, and he winks at me with those crystal balls, also trying to be cheerful-like, but it's terrible.

"Matyusha," he says to me, "we knew each other way back when, and my wife, Nadezhda Vasilyevna—she's lost her mind on account of these times—she was always good to you, you know. And you, Matyusha, you always respected Nadezhda Vasilyevna above anyone. Won't you step in and see her, now that she's lost to the world?"

"All right," I say, and we walk into another room, and there he starts touching my hands, first the right hand, then the left one.

"Matyusha," he says, "are you my fate or what?"

"I'm not," I say. "And get rid of those words. God gave us lackeys the slip—our fate's just a turkey, our life's worth a copeck. So get rid of those words, and listen, if you like, to this letter from Lenin."

"A letter to me, Nikitinsky?"

"To you," and I take out my order book, open it to an empty page, and read, even though I'm illiterate to the depths of my soul.

"*In the name of the people*," I read, "*and for the foundation of a bright future life, I order Pavlichenko, Matvei Rodionych, to deprive various people of life at his discretion…*"

"There it is," I say. "That's Lenin's letter to you…"

And he says to me, "No!"

"No," he says. "Matyusha, although our life's gone to hell and blood's cheap in this Equiapostolic Russian Empire of ours, whatever blood's due to you, you'll get it, and you'll forget all about my dying looks—and wouldn't it better if I showed you my floorboard?"

"Show it," I say. "Maybe it'll be better."

And again we walk across the room, head down into the wine cellar, and there he moves a brick and finds a box behind the brick. There were rings in this box, necklaces, medals and a sacred image done up in pearls. He tosses me the box and stands there, frozen.

"It's yours," he says. "Take what is sacred to the Nikitinskys and walk away, Matvei, to your den in Prikumsk."

That's when I grabbed him, by his throat, by his hair.

"And what about my cheek?" I say. "What do I do about that? How do I live with my cheek, brother?"

And then he laughed, too loud, and didn't try to break free.

"Jackal's conscience," he says and doesn't try to break free. "I'm talking to you like you're an officer of the Russian Empire, but you, louts, were suckled by a she-wolf... Shoot me, then, son of a bitch..."

But I didn't shoot him. I didn't owe him any shooting. I just dragged him up to the big room. Nadezhda Vasilyevna was up there, gone completely crazy. She was holding an unsheathed sabre, kept walking back and forth across the big room and looking in the mirror. But when I dragged Nikitinsky into the room, Nadezhda Vasilyevna ran over to an armchair and sat down. She had a velvet crown on, with feathers sticking out of it. She sat down smart and quick, and presented arms to me with the sabre. And then I stomped my master Nikitinsky. I stomped him for an hour or more than an hour, and in that time I got to know life to its fullest. With shooting—I'll put it this way—with shooting, all you do is get rid of a man. Shooting's a pardon for him, and too damn easy for you. Shooting, it won't get you to the soul—to where it is in a man, how it shows itself. But, when the time comes, I don't spare myself—when the time comes, I stomp the enemy for an hour or more than an hour. I want to get to know life, what life's all about…

# THE CEMETERY IN KOZIN

A CEMETERY in a Jewish shtetl. Assyria and the mysterious decay of the East on the weed-cluttered fields of Volyn. Carved grey stones with three-hundred-year-old inscriptions. The crude embossing of reliefs hewn into the granite. The image of a fish and a sheep over a dead human head. Images of rabbis in fur hats. The rabbis' narrow loins are girded with belts. Beneath their eyeless faces runs a wavy stone line of curly beards. To one side, under an oak crushed by lightning, stands the crypt of Rebbe Azriel, slaughtered by the Cossacks of Bohdan Khmelnytsky.[1] Four generations lie in this tomb, which is as lowly as a water-carrier's hovel, and tablets, greening tablets, sing of them in a Bedouin's prayer:

> Azriel, son of Ananias, mouth of Jehovah.
> Elijah, son of Azriel, mind that entered into
> single combat with oblivion.
> Wolf, son of Elijah, prince abducted from the
> Torah in his nineteenth spring.
> Judah, son of Wolf, Rabbi of Cracow and Prague.
> O death, O profit-seeker, O greedy thief, why
> have you not spared us, even once?

# PRISHCHEPA

I'M MAKING MY WAY to Leszniów, where the division staff has taken up residence. My travelling companion is still Prishchepa—young Kuban Cossack, indefatigable lout, purged communist, future ragpicker, carefree syphilitic and leisurely liar. He's wearing a crimson Circassian coat made of fine cloth and a downy hood thrown over his shoulder. Along the way he told me about himself...

A year ago Prishchepa ran away from the Whites. In retaliation, they took his parents hostage and killed them in the counter-intelligence unit. The neighbours looted their property. When the Whites were driven out of the Kuban, Prishchepa returned to his native village.

It was morning, dawn, peasant sleep sighed in the acrid stuffiness. Prishchepa hired a community cart and went around the village collecting his gramophones, his kvass jugs and the towels his mother had embroidered. He came out into the street in a black cloak, with a curved dagger in his belt, dragging the cart along. Prishchepa went from one neighbour to another, the bloody prints of his soles trailing behind him. In those huts where the Cossack found his mother's things or a chibouk of his father's, he left stabbed old women, dogs hung over the well, icons soiled with dung. The men of the village, puffing at their pipes, followed his path with sullen eyes. The young Cossacks scattered across the steppe, keeping a tally. The tally mounted, and the village was silent. When he was done, Prishchepa returned to his father's devastated home. He set up the recaptured furniture as he'd remembered it standing since childhood and sent for vodka. Shutting himself up in the hut, he drank for two days and nights, sang, cried and hacked at the tables with his sabre. On the third night the village saw smoke over Prishchepa's hut. Singed and ragged, shuffling his feet, he led the cow out of the stall, put a revolver in its mouth and fired. The earth was smoking beneath him, a blue ring of flame flew out of the chimney and melted away, and the abandoned bull calf wailed out in the stable. The fire was as bright as Sunday. Prishchepa untied his horse, jumped into the saddle, threw a lock of his hair into the blaze and vanished.

# THE STORY OF A HORSE

SAVITSKY, our division commander, once took a white stallion from Khlebnikov, commander of the First Squadron. The horse had a magnificent exterior, but its features were raw and always seemed a bit heavy to me. In exchange, Khlebnikov received a little black mare of decent breed, with a smooth trot. But he treated the mare badly, thirsted for vengeance, awaited his chance and finally got it.

After July's unsuccessful battles, when Savitsky was removed from his position and sent back to the reserve ranks of command personnel, Khlebnikov wrote a petition to Army headquarters for the return of his horse. The chief of staff appended the following instructions to the petition: "Said stallion to be restored to his former state." And Khlebnikov, feeling triumphant, covered a hundred *verst*s to find Savitsky, who was then living in Radzivilov, a mutilated little town that looked like a ragged old gossip of a woman. He lived alone, the removed division commander, and the staff's bootlickers no longer recognized him. The staff's bootlickers fished for roast chicken in the Army commander's smiles and, grovelling, turned their backs on the famed division commander.

Bathed in perfume and looking like Peter the Great, he lived in disgrace with Pavla, a Cossack woman he'd won over from a Jewish quartermaster, and twenty thoroughbreds, which we all considered his personal property. The sun in his yard strained and languished with the blinding brightness of its rays; the foals in his yard roughly suckled their dams; grooms with sweaty backs sifted oats on faded fanning mills. Wounded by truth and driven by vengeance, Khlebnikov headed straight for the barricaded yard.

"Are you familiar with my person?" he asked Savitsky, who was lying on some hay.

"Seems I've seen you around," Savitsky answered and yawned.

"Then accept these instructions from the chief of staff," Khlebnikov said firmly. "And I would ask you, comrade from the reserve ranks, to regard me with an official eye…"

"All right," Savitsky murmured soothingly, took the paper and began to read it for an extraordinarily long time. Then he suddenly called to the Cossack woman, who was combing her hair in the cool shade of an awning.

"Pavla," he said. "Lord almighty, we've been combing our hair since morning… Might be nice to get the samovar going…"

The Cossack woman put aside her comb, took her hair in her hands and tossed it behind her back.

"All day long we're after something, Konstantin Vasily-evich," she said with a lazy, imperious grin. "First it's this you want, then that…"

And she went over to the division commander, bearing her breast on high-heeled boots—a breast that moved like an animal in a sack.

"All day long we're after something," the woman repeated, beaming, and buttoned the division commander's shirt over his chest.

"First it's this I want, then that," the division commander laughed, getting up. He wrapped his arm around Pavla's surrendering shoulders and suddenly turned a deathly still face towards Khlebnikov.

"I'm still alive, Khlebnikov," he said, hugging the Cossack woman. "My legs still walk, my horses still gallop, my hands'll still get you and my cannon's warmin' up against my body…"

He drew the revolver that had been resting against his bare stomach and walked up to the commander of the First Squadron.

The latter spun on his heel, spurs whining, and left the yard like an orderly who'd received an urgent dispatch; and again he covered a hundred *verst*s, in order to find the chief of staff, but he turned Khlebnikov away.

"Your case, Commander, is resolved," said the chief of staff. "I have restored your stallion and I've got enough to worry about without you…"

He refused to listen to Khlebnikov and finally returned the truant commander to the First Squadron. Khlebnikov had been away a whole week. During that time we'd been moved to a post in the Dubno woods. We'd pitched our tents there and we lived well. Khlebnikov returned, I remember, on Sunday morning, the 12th. He asked me for more than a quire of paper and ink. The Cossacks planed a tree stump for him; he placed his revolver and the paper on the stump and wrote until evening, scribbling over a multitude of pages.

"A regular Karl Marx," the squadron's military commissar told him that evening. "What the hell are you writing, devil take you?"

"Describing various thoughts in accordance to my oath," Khlebnikov replied, and handed the military commissar his declaration of withdrawal from the Communist Party of Bolsheviks.

"*The Communist Party*," this declaration said, "*was founded, I believe, for happiness and strict justice without limit, and it should also look after the little guy. Now I will touch on the white stallion that I won over from the incredibly counter-revving peasants, that had such a run-down appearance, and many of my comrades laughed at this appearance shamelessly, but I had the strength to bear that harsh laughter and, gritting my teeth for the common cause, I tended that stallion till the desired change, and that's because, comrades, I fancy the white horses, and I put all my strength in them, what little strength is left over from the Imperialist and Civil Wars, and stallions of that sort feel my hand, and I too feel his wordless needs and what's called for, but that unjust black mare is of no need to me; I can't feel her and I can't stand her, as all my comrades can testify, and it might come to grief. And seeing as the party can't restore what's mine to me, in accordance with the chief of staff's instructions, I have no choice but to write out this declaration with tears that don't befit a fighter, but flow on and on and lash at my heart, lashing my heart bloody…*"

This and a lot besides was written in Khlebnikov's declaration. He'd been writing it all day, and it was very long. The military commissar and I struggled with it for about an hour and read it through to the end.

"What a fool," the military commissar said, tearing up the sheets. "Come after supper, you'll have a talk with me."

"Don't need your talk," Khlebnikov replied, trembling. "You've lost me, Military Commissar."

He stood at attention, trembling, without budging, and kept glancing around as if trying to decide which way to run. The military commissar came right up to him, but he didn't see it through. Khlebnikov took off running with all his might.

"Lost me!" he shouted wildly, climbed up on the stump and started ripping at his jacket and clawing at his chest.

"Do it, Savitsky!" he shouted, falling to the ground. "Go ahead and do it!"

We dragged him into a tent; the Cossacks gave us a hand. We boiled tea for him and rolled him cigarettes. He smoked and kept trembling. It wasn't until evening that our commander finally calmed down. He never brought up his foolish declaration again, but a week later he went to Rovno, where he was examined by the medical commission and discharged as an invalid, having sustained six wounds.

And that's how we lost Khlebnikov. This saddened me, because Khlebnikov was a quiet man, similar to me in character. He was the only one in the squadron with a samovar. On days when there was a lull, we'd drink hot tea together. And he'd tell me about women in such detail that, listening to him, I felt ashamed and delighted. I think this was because we were shaken by the same passions. We both looked upon the world as a meadow in May, a meadow traversed by women and horses.

*Radzivilov, July 1920*

# KONKIN

WE WERE CHOPPING the Polish scum down by Belaya Tserkov. Chopping them real fine, with the trees bending and everything. I got hit in the morning, but I was raising plenty of hell, good and proper. The day, I remember, was bowing out to evening. Got carried away from the brigade commander, with no more'n five Cossacks of the proletariat. And all around us, everyone's hacking each other real close, just about hugging, like a priest and his old lady. I've got the sap dripping out of me little by little, my horse's getting wet up front... In a word—two words.

Me and Spirka Zabuty hightail it out of there, away from the woods. We look up and see some numbers we like... 'Bout three hundred *sazhen*s off, no more'n that, it's either the staff kicking up dust, or the transport. If it's the staff, good—if it's the transport, even better. The boys' rags are all tattered, shirts don't even reach their sexual maturity.

"Zabuty," I say to Spirka. "Up your mother's you-know-what and the like—well, I leave it you, you're the official orator—if that ain't their staff moving out..."

"Sure thing, their staff," says Spirka. "Only it's two of us and eight of them..."

"The hell with it, Spirka," I say. "I'll still get their robes dirty… We'll die for a pickle and world revolution…"

And off we went. There were eight sabres in all. We picked two of 'em off right away with our rifles. I see Spirka's dragging a third to Dukhonin's headquarters to check his papers.[1] But I'm aiming for the ace. He was a crimson ace, boys—gold watch on a chain and everything. I run him down to a farm. Farm had apples and cherries all over it. My ace has a horse under him like a merchant's daughter, but it's worn out. So the Pan General drops the reins, trains his Mauser on me and makes a hole in my leg.

"All right," I think, "you're mine, sweetheart—you'll spread those legs."

I go flat out and plant two rounds in the little horse. I was sorry about that stallion. A little Bolshevik, that stallion was—a regular little Bolshevik. All coppery like a coin, tail like a bullet, legs like bowstrings. Thought I'd bring him to Lenin alive, but it didn't work out. I liquidated that little horse. It tumbled like a bride, and my ace came out of the saddle. He took off running, but then he turned around again and made another draught-hole in my figure. So now I've got three decorations for action against the enemy.

"Jesus," I think. "He might go and kill me on accident…"

So I gallop up to him, and he's already got his sword out, tears running down his cheeks, white tears, human milk.

"You're gonna get me the Order of the Red Banner!" I shout. "Surrender, Most Illustrious, while I'm still alive!…"

"*Nie moge, Pan*,"[2] the old man answers. "You'll cut me down…"

And suddenly Spiridon's in my face, like a leaf in the grass. He's all lathered up, with his eyes dangling on strings from his mug.

"Vasya," he shouts to me, "you won't believe how many I've finished off today! But that's a general you've got, he's got the trimmings on him, and I'd like to finish him off."

"Go to the Turk!" I tell Zabuty, getting cross. "Those trimmings of his cost me blood."

And I run the general into a barn with my mare. There was hay in there or something. It was quiet there, dark, cool.

"Pan," I say, "calm your old self down, surrender, for God's sake, and you and I can both have a rest, Pan…"

But he's panting against the wall, rubbing his forehead with a red finger.

"*Nie moge*," he says. "You'll cut me down. I'll only give up my sabre to Budyonny…"

I should get him Budyonny. Just my luck! And I see the old man's done for.

"Pan," I shout, wailing and gnashing my teeth, "I give you a proletarian's word, I'm commander-in-chief around here. Don't look for the trimmings on me, but I've got the title. Here's the title: musical eccentric and salon ventriloquist from Nizhny… The town of Nizhny on the Volga River…"

And the devil worked me up into a lather. The general's eyes blinked like lanterns in front of me. A red sea opened up in front of me. Resentment worked its way into my wound like salt, 'cause I see that grandpa don't believe me. So I closed my mouth, boys, pulled in my belly, took in some air, and heaped it on 'im the old fashioned way, our way, the fighters' way, the Nizhny Novgorod way, and I proved to that Polish scum what a ventriloquist I was.

So then the old man went white, grabbed at his heart and sat down on the ground.

"Now d'you believe Vaska the eccentric, commissar of the Third Invincible Cavalry Brigade?…"

"Commissar?" he shouts.

"Commissar," I say.

"Communist?" he shouts.

"Communist," I say.

"In my dying hour," he shouts, "as I take my final breath, tell me, my Cossack friend—are you a communist or are you lying?"

"I'm a communist," I say.

So my grandpa sits on the ground, kisses some sort of amulet, breaks his sabre in half and two lamps go on in his eyes, two lanterns above the dark steppe.

"Forgive me," he says. "I cannot surrender to a communist." And he shakes my hand. "Forgive me," he says, "and hack me down like a soldier…"

This story was told to us during a halt, by Konkin, political commissar of the N—— Cavalry Brigade and three-time recipient of the Order of the Red Banner, with all his usual buffoonery.

"And what did you and the Pan agree to, Vaska?"

"What can you agree to, with a fellow like that?... Had too much honour in him. I even bowed to him, but he wouldn't give. So we took whatever papers he had on him, took the Mauser—the old crank's saddle's still under me to this day. And then I see more and more blood's dripping out of me, there's an awful sleepiness coming over me, my boots are full of blood—I'm not thinking of him..."

"So you put the old man out of his misery then?"

"Sad to say."

# BERESTECHKO

WE WERE MARCHING over from Khotin to Berestechko. The fighters dozed in their high saddles. A song gurgled in the air like a creek running dry. Monstrous corpses littered millennia-old burial mounds. White-shirted peasants pulled off their caps and bowed as we passed. Division Commander Pavlichenko's felt cloak fluttered over the staff like a sombre flag. His downy hood was thrown over his cloak, and his curved sabre hung at his side as if it were glued there.

We rode past the Cossack burial mounds and Bohdan Khmelnytsky's tower. An old man crept out from behind a gravestone with a bandura and, in a childlike voice, sang of bygone Cossack glory. We listened to his song in silence, then unfurled our banners and burst into Berestechko to the sound of a thundering march. The residents had put iron bars over their shutters; sovereign silence ascended her shtetl throne.

I found myself billeted with a red-headed widow, who reeked of a widow's grief. I washed off the road's dust and went out into the street. Announcements were posted that Vinogradov, the division's military commissar, would read a report that evening on the Second Congress of the

Comintern. Right in front of my window some Cossacks were trying to shoot an old Jew with a silvery beard for espionage. The old man was squealing, struggling to break free. Then Kudrya from the machine-gun detachment took his head and stuck it under his arm. The Jew went quiet and spread his legs. Kudrya drew his dagger with his right hand and carefully stabbed the old man, without splattering himself. Then he knocked on the closed window frame.

"If anyone's interested," he said, "let 'em come and get 'im. Fine by me…"

Then the Cossacks turned the corner. I followed them and began roaming Berestechko. It's mostly Jews here, but Russian tradesmen—leather-tanners—have settled on the outskirts. They live neatly, in white houses behind green shutters. Instead of vodka, the tradesmen drink beer or mead; they grow tobacco in their front gardens and smoke it in long, bent chibouks, like Galician peasants. Living in close quarters with three tribes, all industrious and businesslike, awoke in them a stubborn diligence, which is sometimes characteristic of the Russian, when he has not yet gone lousy, given in to despair and lost himself to drink.

The old way of life had been driven out of Berestechko, but it was steadfast here. Shoots three centuries old still grew green with the warm rot of antiquity in Volyn. Here, with the thread of profit, Jews bound the Russian peasant to the Polish Pan, the Czech settler with the factory in Łódź. These were smugglers, the finest on the frontier, and almost always warriors for the faith. Hasidism held this bustling population of tavern keepers, pedlars and brokers in stifling captivity. Boys in kaftans still trampled the age-old road to the Hasidic *cheder*, and old women still brought brides to the *tsaddik* with fervent prayers for fertility.

Jews live here in spacious houses smeared with white or watery-blue paint. The traditional poverty of this architecture goes back centuries. Behind each house is a shed, reaching two, sometimes three, storeys in height. It never lets in any sun. These indescribably gloomy sheds take the place of our yards. Secret passages lead to cellars and stables. In wartime these catacombs hide people from bullets and looting. Over many days, human waste and cattle dung pile up. Despondency and terror fill the catacombs with the acrid stench and foul sourness of excrement.

Berestechko stinks inviolably to this day. All the people here give off the stench of rotten herring. The shtetl reeks in anticipation of a new era; what one sees isn't people, but faded schemes of frontier misfortunes. I was sick of them by the end of the day. I walked past the city limits, climbed a hill and penetrated the devastated castle of the Counts Raciborski, the recent owners of Berestechko.

The calm of sunset turned the grass around the castle blue. The moon, green as a lizard, rose over the pond. From the window I could see the estate of the Counts Raciborski— meadows and plantations of hops, concealed by the moiré ribbons of dusk.

A mad ninety-year-old countess used to live in the castle with her son. She plagued her son for not giving the vanishing clan any heirs, and—the peasants told me—the countess would beat her son with a coachman's whip.

A rally was gathering on the square below. It drew peasants, Jews and tanners from the outskirts. Above them flared Vinogradov's enthusiastic voice and the clank of his spurs. He spoke of the Second Congress of the Comintern, while I roamed along walls on which nymphs with gouged-out eyes performed an ancient round dance. Then, in a corner, on the muddied floor, I found a fragment of a yellowed letter. Its faded ink read:

*Berestetchko, 1820. Paul, mon bien aimé, on dit que l'empereur Napoléon est mort, est-ce vrai? Moi, je me sens bien, les couches ont été faciles, notre petit héros achève sept semaines…*[1]

Down below, the voice of the division's military commissar blares on. He is passionately trying to convince the puzzled tradesmen and plundered Jews:

"You are the power. Everything here is yours. There are no Pans. I now proceed to the election of the Revolutionary Committee…"

# SALT

"**D**EAR COMRADE EDITOR. I want to describe a thing or two about thoughtless women, who do us harm. The boys trust that when you were making your rounds on the Civil Front, which you took note of, you didn't pass over the hopeless station of Fastov, which sits at the end of the earth, in a land far, far away, address unknown—sure enough I was there, drank home-brewed beer, got my whiskers all wet, but my mouth's still dry. Now, I could write plenty about this above-mentioned station, but as they say in our simple way—you won't clear the master's shit pile. So I'll describe to you only what my own eyes have seen first-hand.

"It was a nice, quiet little night seven days ago, when our esteemed Red Cavalry train stopped there, loaded up with fighting boys. We were all fired up to contribute to the common cause and had Berdichev as our destination. Only we notice our train's not moving, our little rascal's not turning, and the fighters get to doubting, talking—what's this stop all about? And sure enough this turned out to be one hell of a stop for the common cause, all on account of the profiteers, those evil enemies with untold numbers of the female sex among them, who were getting impudent with the railroad authorities. Without a hint of fear, they latched onto the handrails, yes, these evil enemies darted across the iron roofs, running riot and stirring up trouble, and each hand featured the notorious salt, up to five *pood*s a sack. But the capitalist profiteers' triumph didn't last long. The initiative of the fighting boys, who came climbing out of the carriages, gave the outraged railroad authorities a chance to breathe. Only the female sex stuck around, with its sacks. The fighters took pity—they put some women in the goods vans, some they didn't. That's how two girls ended up with us, in the Second Platoon's carriage. And as soon as we hear the first bell, up comes a respectable-looking woman with a child, saying:

"'Let me on, kind Cossack boys. This whole war I've suffered at railroad stations, with a nursing child in my arms, and now I want to see my husband, but you can't get anywhere on account of the railroad. Don't I deserve better, Cossack boys?'

"'Let me tell you, woman,' I say, 'whatever the platoon agrees to, that'll be your fate.' And, turning to the platoon, I argue that a respectable-looking woman is asking to see her husband at our destination, and that she really has a child with her, and what will you agree to—let her on or no?

"'Let her on,' the lads yell. 'After we're through, she won't be wanting her husband!…'

"'No,' I tell the lads quite politely. 'I bow to you, platoon, but I'm surprised to hear that kind of horseplay out of you. Remember your lives, platoon, and how you too were children in your mothers' arms, and talk like this—well, it just won't do…'

"And the Cossacks—after talking it over some, saying what a persuasive fellow that Balmashov is—start letting the woman into the carriage, and she clambers up gratefully. And they're all worked up by my truth, trying to help her up, vying with one another:

"'Please sit, woman, in the corner there, and tend to your child the way mothers do, no one will touch you in the corner, and you'll get to your husband untouched, just like you wanted, and we're depending on your conscience to bring up some new blood for us, 'cause the old are getting older and the young, you see, are hard to come by. We've seen plenty of grief, woman, when we were drafted and when we re-enlisted, pressed by hunger, blistered by the cold. But you sit here, woman, and don't you worry…'

"And when the third bell sounded, the train moved. And the nice little night pitched its tent. And in that tent hung star-lanterns. And the boys remembered the Kuban night and the green Kuban star. And a song flew by, like a bird. And the wheels went on rumbling, rumbling…

"After some time, when the night was relieved from its post and the red drummers were tapping out reveille on their red drums, the Cossacks came up to me, because they saw I was sitting there, sleepless and sad as can be.

"'Balmashov,' the Cossacks say, 'what's got you so sad, sitting there sleepless?'

"'I bow low to you, fighters, and ask a little forgiveness, but let me have a few words with that nursing citizen there…'

"And I get up from my resting place, from which sleep ran like a wolf from a pack of villainous dogs, and I walk up to her, trembling from head to toe, and I take her child from her hands and tear the swaddling clothes off it, and I see it's a good *pood* of salt.

"'Now here's a curious child, comrades, that don't ask for the teat, don't pee on the skirt and don't trouble your sleep…'

"'Forgive me, kind Cossack boys,' the woman butts into our conversation, all cool-headed. 'I didn't lie to you; it's my grief that lied to you…'

"'Balmashov, he'll forgive your grief,' I answer the woman. 'It doesn't cost him much. Balmashov sells it for what he bought it. But take a look at the Cossacks, woman, who raised you up as a toiling mother of the republic. Take a look at these two girls, who're crying now, on account of how they suffered from us in the night. Take a look at our wives, wasting their womanly strength out in the Kuban wheat fields, with their husbands gone, and those husbands, just as lonely, forced by evil need to rape girls that cross their path… But you—they didn't touch you, though you're just the one they should've touched, you wretch. Take a look at Russia, crushed by pain…'

"And she says to me:

"'I've lost my salt, and truth don't scare me. You don't care a thing about Russia, you're saving those Yids, Lenin and Trotsky…'

"'We aren't talking Yids, vile citizen. Yids have nothing to do with it. By the way, I don't know about Lenin, but Trotsky's the daredevil son of a Tambov governor, and he went over to the working class, though he comes from another. They drag us out—Lenin and Trotsky—like condemned convicts onto the free path of life, but you, foul citizen, are more counter-revolutionary than that White general who threatens us with his sharp sabre on his thousand-rouble horse… That general, you can see him on every road, and the worker dreams of cutting him down, but you, deceitful citizen, with your curious children who don't ask for bread and don't do their business—you're hard for the eye to see, like a flea, and you bite, and bite, and bite…'

"And I admit it, I do—I tossed that citizen off the moving train, right on the embankment, but being a rough one, she just sat there a while, flapped her skirts and went on her crooked little way. And seeing this unharmed woman, with unspeakable Russia all around her, and peasant fields without an ear of wheat, and the outraged girls, and my comrades who ride off to the front all the time but don't come back much, I had a mind to jump from the carriage and either finish myself off or finish her off. But the Cossacks had pity on me and said:

"'Hit her with the rifle.'

"And taking my trusty rifle off the wall, I washed that shame from the face of the workers' land and of the republic.

"And we, the fighters of the Second Platoon, swear to you, dear Comrade Editor, and to you, dear comrades of the editorial board, to deal mercilessly with all the traitors who drag us into the pit, who want to turn back the river and pave Russia with corpses and dead grass.

"For all the fighters of the Second Platoon—Nikita Balmashov, soldier of the revolution."

# EVENING

O CHARTER of the Russian Communist Party! You've laid headlong rails through the sour dough of Russian tales. You've turned three idle hearts, brimming with the passions of Ryazan Christs, into contributors to *The Red Cavalryman*—turned them so that each day they could compose the rollicking newspaper, full of courage and crude joy.

The wall-eyed Galin, the consumptive Slinkin and Sychov, with his ulcerated gut, roam about in the barren dust of the rear and spread the riot and fire of their leaflets through the ranks of hardy Cossacks relieved from the front, crooks in the reserve listed as Polish interpreters, and girls sent to our political-department train from Moscow for a good rest.

The newspaper—that detonating cord laid under the army—is only finished at nightfall. The squint-eyed lantern of the provincial sun goes out in the sky; the lights of the printing press, flying every which way, flare uncontrollably, like the passion of a machine. Then, at about midnight, Galin steps out of the carriage to shudder at the stings of his unrequited love for our train's washerwoman, Irina.

"Last time," says Galin, narrow-shouldered, pale and blind. "Last time, Irina, we covered the execution of Nicholas the Bloody, put to death by the Yekaterinburg proletariat. Now we'll move on to other tyrants who died like dogs. Peter III was strangled by Orlov, his wife's lover. Paul was torn apart by courtiers, and by his own son. Nicholas the Rod poisoned himself, his son fell on the first of March, his grandson died of drink... You need to know all this, Irina..."[1]

And fixing the washerwoman with his naked eye, full of adoration, Galin tirelessly stirs the crypts of fallen emperors. He stands stooped, doused by the moon that's stuck up there like an insolent splinter; the printing machines clatter away somewhere close by and the radio station shines with a pure light. Nestling up against the cook Vasily's shoulder, Irina listens to the dull and senseless muttering of love. Above her head, stars trudge through the sky's black seaweed. The washerwoman dozes, makes the sign of the Cross over her puffy lips and looks at Galin wide-eyed. This is how a young girl who longs for the nuisance of conception looks at a professor devoted to science.

Next to Irina yawns the heavy-jowled Vasily, who, like all cooks, despises mankind. Cooks—they're always dealing with the meat of dead animals and the greed of the living, which is why cooks look for things in politics that don't concern them. So it was with Vasily, the heavy-jowled conqueror. Pulling his trousers up to his nipples, he asks Galin about the civil lists of various kings, about the dowry for the tsar's daughter, and then he says, yawning:

"It's night time, Rina. And we've got a day tomorrow. Let's go crush some fleas…"

And they closed the door to the kitchen, leaving Galin alone with the moon, sticking up there like an insolent splinter… Facing the moon, on a slope by a sleeping pond, I sat in my glasses, with boils on my neck and bandaged legs. I was digesting the class struggle in my vague poetic brains when Galin came up to me with his gleaming wall-eyes.

"Galin," I said, stricken with self-pity and loneliness. "I'm sick, seems my end is near, and I'm tired of living in our Red Cavalry…"

"You're a wimp," said Galin, and the watch on his skinny wrist showed one o'clock in the morning. "You're a wimp, and we're fated to suffer you wimps… The whole Party is walking around in aprons smeared with blood and excrement—we're taking the shell off the kernel for you. Not long from now, you'll see the shelled kernel, take your finger out of your nose and sing praises to the new life in extraordinary prose, but meanwhile sit quiet, wimp, and don't get in the way with your whining…"

He leant closer to me, adjusted the bandages that had come loose on my scabby sores, and hung his head on his pigeon chest. Night comforted us in our sorrows, a light breeze fanned us like a mother's skirt, and the grasses below glistened with freshness and moisture.

The machines thundering in the train's printing press screeched and fell silent, dawn drew a line at the edge of the earth, and the door to the kitchen whistled and opened a crack. Four legs with fat heels were thrust out into the cool, and we saw Irina's loving calves and Vasily's big toe, with its crooked black nail.

"Vasilyok," the woman whispered in an intimate, languishing Russian voice. "Get out of my bed, you troublemaker…"

But Vasily only jerked his heel and moved closer.

"The cavalry," Galin then said to me. "The cavalry is a social trick effected by the Central Committee of our Party. The curve of the Revolution has thrown Cossack freebooters, soaked through with many prejudices, into the front rank, but the Central Committee, manoeuvring, will rake through them with an iron brush…"

And Galin started talking about the political education of the First Cavalry. He spoke for a long time, dully, with complete clarity. His lid twitched over his wall-eye and blood ran from his lacerated palms.

*Kovel, 1920*

# AFONKA BIDA

WE WERE FIGHTING at Leszniów. The wall of the enemy's cavalry kept appearing on all sides of us. The coiled spring of the fortified Polish strategy stretched out with an ominous whistle. We were being pressed. For the first time during the whole campaign we felt on our back the devilish sting of flank attacks and breaches in the rear—bites from the very same weapons that had served us so happily.

The infantry held the front at Leszniów. Along crookedly dug trenches hunkered the blond, barefoot peasants of Volyn. This infantry was taken from the plough the day before, so as to form a reserve for the Red Cavalry. The peasants went willingly. They fought with the utmost diligence. Even Budyonny's men were amazed at their snorting peasant ferocity. Their hatred for the Polish landowner was built of plain but sturdy material.

In the second phase of the war, when whooping had ceased to affect the opponent's imagination and horseback attacks on the entrenched enemy had become impossible, this home-made infantry would have proved of the utmost benefit to the Red Cavalry. But our poverty prevailed. The peasants were given one rifle between three, and cartridges that didn't fit. The venture had to be abandoned, and this genuine people's guard was disbanded and sent home.

Now let us turn to the fighting at Leszniów. The foot soldiers had dug in about three *verst*s from town. Ahead of their frontline walked a stoop-shouldered young man wearing glasses. A sabre dragged at his side. He moved with a skipping step, looking displeased, as if his boots were pinching him. This peasant ataman,[1] their chosen one, their favourite, was a Jew, a purblind youth with the sallow and focused face of a Talmudist. In battle he displayed a circumspect courage and composure that somewhat resembled the absent-mindedness of a dreamer.

It was the third hour of an expansive July afternoon. Heat's iridescent gossamer shimmered in the air. Behind the hills flashed a festive stripe of full-dress uniforms and horses' manes braided with ribbons. The young man gave the signal to get ready. The peasants ran to their positions, their bast shoes slapping on the ground, and held their guns at the ready. But the alarm turned out to be false. It was Maslak's[2] florid squadrons that came out on the Leszniów highway. Their emaciated but lively steeds moved at a round pace. Lush banners on gilt staffs burdened with velvet tassels swayed in fiery pillars of dust. The horsemen rode with majestic and insolent coldness. The shaggy foot soldiers crawled out of their trenches and stared, slack-jawed, at the taut elegance of this unhurried stream.

At the head of the regiment, on a bow-legged steppe nag, rode Brigade Commander Maslak, full of drunken blood and the rot of his own fatty juices. His belly lay on the silver-bound pommel like a big tomcat. Catching sight of the foot soldiers, Maslak flushed gaily and beckoned to Afonka Bida, the platoon commander. We had nicknamed the platoon commander "Makhno", on account of his resemblance to the old man. They whispered for a moment, the brigade commander and Afonka. Then the platoon commander turned to the First Squadron, leant forward and quietly ordered: "Reins!" The Cossack platoon moved into a trot. They whipped up the horses and raced towards the trenches, from which the foot soldiers gaped, delighted by the spectacle.

"Prepare for battle!" Afonka's mournful voice sang out, as if from far away.

Wheezing, coughing and enjoying himself, Maslak rode off to the side. The Cossacks rushed to the attack. The poor foot soldiers ran, but it was too late. The Cossack lashes had already fallen on their ragged sackcloth. The riders circled the field and twirled their whips with extraordinary artistry.

"What are you fooling around for?" I shouted to Afonka.

"For a laugh," he replied, fidgeting in his saddle and pulling out a lad who'd been hiding in the bushes.

"For a laugh!" he cried, poking at the unconscious lad.

The fun ended when Maslak, grown soft and magnanimous, waved his plump hand.

"Stop your yawning, foot soldiers!" Afonka cried and haughtily straightened his feeble body. "Go and catch some fleas, foot soldiers…"

The Cossacks, exchanging smiles, assembled in ranks. The foot soldiers had vanished without a trace. The trenches were empty. And only the stoop-shouldered Jew remained standing in the same place, peering disdainfully at the Cossacks through his glasses.

There was no break in the shooting coming from Leszniów. The Poles were surrounding us. Through binoculars one could see the individual figures of mounted scouts. They'd hop out of the town and fall back in, like roly-polies. Maslak formed a squadron and scattered it on both sides of the highway. The sky that rose above Leszniów was brilliant and inexpressibly empty, as always in hours of peril. The Jew, throwing back his head, whistled mournfully and mightily on his metal pipe. And the foot soldiers, those unique, rough-hewn foot soldiers, returned to their places.

Bullets were flying thick in our direction. The brigade staff came under machine-gun fire. We bolted into the woods and began to claw our way through the bushes that lay to the right of the highway. Shot-up branches groaned above us. When we'd made it out of the bushes, the Cossacks were no longer where they'd been. By order of the division commander, they were retreating towards Brody. There was no one left but the peasants, snarling from their trenches with sparse rifle shots, and the straggler Afonka, chasing after his platoon.

He was riding on the very edge of the road, looking around and sniffing at the air. The shooting died down for a moment. The Cossack thought to take advantage of the lull and broke into a full gallop. At that instant a bullet pierced his horse's neck. Afonka rode on another hundred paces or so, and then, right in our midst, his horse abruptly bent its forelegs and fell to the ground.

Afonka slowly pulled his crushed foot out of the stirrup. He squatted down and poked a copper-coloured finger into the wound. Then Bida straightened up and surveyed the gleaming horizon with agonized eyes.

"Goodbye, Stepan," he said in a wooden voice, stepped away from the dying animal and bowed to it from the waist. "How will I come back to the quiet village without you?... What will I do with your embroidered saddle? Goodbye, Stepan," he repeated more forcefully, choked up, squeaked like a trapped mouse and commenced wailing. The gurgling wail reached our ears, and we saw Afonka bowing and bowing, like a hysterical woman in church. "I won't give in to greedy fate, damn it," he shouted, removing his hands from his face, which was stiff with grief. "I'll hack down the unspeakable Poles—no mercy! Till my heart gives out, till their last gasp and the Mother of God's blood... I make you a promise before all the men from the village, all my dear brothers, Stepan..."

Afonka lay down with his face in the wound and fell silent. Fixing its deep, shining, violet eye on its master, the horse listened to Afonka's broken wheezing. It drew its muzzle over the ground in gentle oblivion, and streams of blood, like two ruby breast-bands, trickled down the white muscles of its chest.

Afonka lay without stirring. Maslak minced over to the horse on his fat legs, placed a revolver in its ear, and fired.

Afonka leapt up and turned his terrible, pockmarked face to Maslak.

"Gather up the harness, Afanasy," Maslak said tenderly. "Head over to your unit…"

And from the slope we saw Afonka, bent beneath the saddle's weight, with a face as wet and red as cleaved meat, plodding his way over to his squadron, immeasurably lonely in the dusty, blazing desert of the fields.

Late in the evening I came across him in the unit transport. He was sleeping on a cart that held all his possessions—sabres, service jackets and pierced gold coins. The platoon commander's blood-caked head, with its lifeless, contorted mouth, lolled as if crucified on the bend of his saddle. Next to him lay the dead horse's harness, the intricate and frilly garb of a Cossack racer—breast-collars with black tassels, pliant cruppers studded with coloured stones, and a bridle embossed with silver.

The darkness was bearing down on us, growing ever thicker. The transport dragged out along the Brody highway; simple little stars rolled through the milky ways of the sky, and far-off villages burnt in the cool depths of the night. Orlov, the squadron commander's assistant, and the long-whiskered Bitsenko were sitting there on Afonka's cart and discussing his grief.

"He brought that steed from home," said the long-whiskered Bitsenko. "Where you gonna find a steed like that?"

"A steed's a friend," replied Orlov.

"A steed's a father," sighed Bitsenko. "Saves your life more'n you can count. Bida's done for without a steed…"

And by the morning Afonka had disappeared. The fighting at Brody began and ended. Defeat gave way to temporary victory, we saw our division commander relieved and replaced, but Afonka was nowhere to be seen. And only the ominous grumbling hanging over the villages—the vicious, predatory trail of Afonka's freebooting—pointed us to his difficult path.

"Procuring a steed," the men in the squadron said about the platoon commander, and on the vast evenings of our wanderings I heard plenty of stories about this lonely, ferocious procurement.

Men from other units would stumble upon Afonka dozens of *verst*s from our position. He'd be lurking in ambush for straggling Polish cavalrymen or scouring the woods for herds of horses hidden by peasants. He'd set villages on fire and shoot Polish headmen for concealment. Echoes of this furious solitary combat would reach our ears—echoes of a lone wolf's desperate, thievish attacks on a colossus.

Another week passed. The bitter anger of the day drove stories of Afonka's gloomy daring out of circulation, and we began to forget about "Makhno". Then came a rumour that he'd been slaughtered by Galician peasants someplace in the woods. And on the day of our entry into Berestechko, Yemelyan Budyak of the First Squadron went to the division commander to ask for Afonka's saddle with its yellow cloth. Yemelyan wanted to ride out for review with a new saddle, but this was not to be.

We entered Berestechko on 6 August. At the head of our division advanced the Asiatic tunic and red Cossack coat of the new division commander. Behind him came Lyovka, the crazed lackey, leading the stud mare. A battle march, full of prolonged menace, flew along the fanciful, beggarly streets. Tumbledown alleys, a painted forest of decrepit and trembling cross-beams, ran the length of the town. Its core, eaten away by time, breathed a melancholy decay upon us. The smugglers and hypocrites had taken refuge in their dark, spacious huts. Only Pan Ludomirski, the bell-ringer in his green frock coat, greeted us at the church.

We crossed the river and went deep into the tradesmen's settlement. We were approaching the priest's house when Afonka came riding round the corner on a strapping grey stallion.

"My respects!" he pronounced in a barking voice and, pushing the fighters aside, took his place in the ranks.

Maslak gazed off into the colourless distance. Without turning round, he wheezed:

"Where did you get the steed?"

"It's my own," replied Afonka, then rolled a cigarette and moistened it with a quick flick of his tongue.

The Cossacks were riding up to greet him one by one. On his charred face, a monstrous pink swelling gaped repulsively in place of a left eye.

And the next morning Bida went on a spree. He smashed St Valentine's shrine in the church and tried to play the organ. He wore a jacket cut from a blue carpet, with a lily embroidered on the back, and his sweaty forelock was combed over his gouged-out eye.

After lunch he saddled his horse and fired his rifle at the broken windows of the castle of the Counts Raciborski. The Cossacks stood around him in a semicircle... They were lifting the stallion's tail, groping its legs and counting its teeth.

"A solid steed," said Orlov, the squadron commander's assistant.

"A sound horse," confirmed the long-whiskered Bitsenko.

# IN ST VALENTINE'S

O UR DIVISION OCCUPIED Berestechko yesterday
evening. The staff set itself up in the house of the priest
Tuzinkiewicz. Disguised as a peasant woman, Tuzinkiewicz
fled Berestechko before our troops entered the town. What
I know about him is that he'd spent forty-five years potter-
ing about with God in Berestechko and was a good priest.
When the residents want us to understand this, they tell us
he was loved by the Jews. Under Tuzinkiewicz, the ancient
church was renovated. They finished the repairs on the day
of the temple's tercentenary. The bishop had come out from
Zhitomir for the occasion. Prelates in silk cassocks held a
service in front of the church. Pot-bellied and blissful, they
stood like bells in the dewy grass. Duteous rivers flowed in
from the surrounding villages. Peasants bent their knees,
kissed priests' hands, and that same day such clouds flamed
in the heavens as had never been seen before. The banners
of heaven were waving in honour of the old church. The
bishop himself kissed Tuzinkiewicz on the forehead and
called him the father of Berestechko, *pater Béresteckea*.

I heard this story in the morning at headquarters, where
I was going over the report of our flank column, which was

reconnoitring around Lwów in the district of Radziechów. I was reading the documents, and the snoring of the orderlies behind my back spoke of our never-ending homelessness. The clerks, damp from a lack of sleep, were writing out orders for the division, eating cucumbers and sneezing. It was only by midday that I was free, walked over to the window and saw the temple of Berestechko—mighty and white. It glowed in the cool sun, like a delftware tower. Midday lightning bolts sparkled in its glossy sides. Their convex lines began at the ancient green colour of the cupolas and ran lightly downward. Pink veins glimmered in the white stone of the pediment, while at the top stood columns as slender as candles.

Then the singing of the organ struck my ears, and at that very moment an old woman with loose yellow hair appeared on the threshold of headquarters. She moved like a dog with a broken paw, circling and lurching to the ground. Her pupils, poured full of the white moisture of blindness, were sprinkling tears. The sounds of the organ, now ponderous, now hurried, floated over to us. Their flight was difficult, and their trail rang long and plaintively. The old woman wiped her tears with her yellow hair, sat down on the ground and started kissing my boots at the knee. The organ fell silent and then burst out laughing in bass notes. I grabbed the old woman by the arm and looked around. The clerks were tapping at typewriters; the orderlies snored all the louder, their spurs cutting the thick felt beneath the velvet upholstery of the couches. The old woman was kissing my boots tenderly, embracing them as she would an infant. I dragged her outside and locked the door behind me. The church stood before us, as dazzling as a stage set. Its side gates were open, and the graves of Polish officers were strewn with horse skulls.

We ran into the yard, walked through a gloomy corridor and ended up in a square room attached to the chancel. Sashka, a nurse of the Thirty-First Regiment, was running things in there. She was rummaging through silks that someone had thrown on the floor. The deathly aroma of brocade, crushed flowers and fragrant decay poured into her quivering nostrils, tickling and poisoning them. Then some Cossacks came into the room. They burst out laughing, grabbed Sashka by the hand and tossed her with all their might onto the mountain of fabrics and books. Sashka's body, flowering and reeking like the meat of a freshly slaughtered cow, was laid bare; her hiked-up skirts exposed the legs of a squadron woman—shapely, cast-iron legs—and Kudryukov, a doltish youngster, straddled Sashka and bounced as if in a saddle, pretending to be overcome with passion. She threw him off and ran to the door. And only then, after passing the altar, did we penetrate into the church.

It was full of light, this church—full of dancing rays, airy columns, some kind of cool joy. How can I ever forget the picture that hung over the right bye-altar and was painted by Apolek? In this picture, twelve pink *paters* are rocking a chubby infant Jesus in a cradle entwined with ribbons. His toes stick out, and his body is lacquered by the hot sweat of morning. The child is rolling on his fatty back, which is gathered into folds; the twelve apostles, in cardinals' tiaras, are bent over the cradle. Their faces are shaved blue and their fiery cloaks stick out over their bellies. The apostles' eyes sparkle with wisdom, determination, joy; thin smiles play at the corners of their mouths, and flame-coloured warts are planted on their double chins—crimson warts, like radishes in May.

In this temple of Berestechko there was a singular, seductive point of view on the mortal sufferings of the sons of men. In this temple the saints marched off to their deaths with the picturesqueness of Italian singers, and the executioners' black hair glistened like the beard of Holofernes. There too, above the royal doors, I beheld a blasphemous image of John belonging to the heretical and intoxicating brush of Apolek. In this image the baptist was beautiful, with that ambiguous, unspoken beauty over which the concubines of kings lose their half-lost honour and blossoming lives.

Driven mad by the memory of my desire, the memory of Apolek, I didn't notice the traces of destruction in the church, or they seemed insignificant to me. It was only the shrine of St Valentine that was broken. Tufts of decayed wadding lay about underneath it, along with the laughable bones of the saint, resembling chicken bones more than anything. And Afonka Bida was still playing the organ. He was drunk, Afonka, wild and gashed all over. He'd only come back to us the day before, with a horse he'd won over from the peasants. Afonka was stubbornly trying to pick out a march on the organ, and someone was urging him in a sleepy voice: "Drop it, Afonka, let's go and feed." But the Cossack wouldn't drop it, and there was a multitude of them—Afonka's songs. Each sound was a song, and all the sounds were cut off from one another. A song—its dense strain—would last a moment and pass into another... I listened, gazing around, and the traces of destruction seemed insignificant to me. But Pan Ludomirski, the bell-ringer of the Church of St Valentine and the blind old woman's husband, thought otherwise.

Ludomirski had crept out of nowhere. He walked into the church at a steady pace with his head down. The old man couldn't bring himself to throw a covering over the scattered relics, because a commoner isn't permitted to touch a sacred object. The bell-ringer fell onto the light-blue tile of the floor, lifted his head, and his blue nose rose over him like a flag over a corpse. The blue nose trembled above him; at that moment, the velvet curtain at the altar rippled and, trembling, crept back to one side. In the depths of the opened niche, against the background of a sky furrowed by clouds, ran a bearded little figure in an orange *kontusz*[1]—barefoot, with a lacerated, bleeding mouth. And then a hoarse howl ripped through our ears. We retreated, incredulous, in the face of horror; horror overtook us and probed our hearts with dead fingers. I saw that the man in the orange *kontusz* was being pursued by hatred and overtaken by the chase. He had bent his arm to ward off an impending blow, and blood spilt from the arm in a purple current. The little Cossack standing next to me cried out and, lowering his head, ran off, though there was nothing to run from, because the figure in the niche was merely Jesus Christ—the most extraordinary image of God that I have ever seen in my life.

Pan Ludomirski's Saviour was a curly little Yid with a small, scraggly beard and a low, wrinkled forehead. His sunken cheeks were painted with carmine, and thin ginger eyebrows arched over the eyes closed in pain.

His mouth was lacerated, like a horse's lip, his Polish *kontusz* was girdled by an expensive belt, and under the caftan writhed little porcelain feet—painted, bare and pierced with silver nails.

Pan Ludomirski stood under the statue in his green frock coat. He stretched his withered hand above our heads and cursed us. The Cossacks opened their eyes wide and hung their straw-coloured forelocks. In a thunderous voice the bell-ringer of the Church of St Valentine anathematized us in the purest Latin. Then he turned away, fell to his knees and embraced the Saviour's legs.

When I returned to headquarters, I wrote a report to the division commander concerning this insult to the religious feelings of the local population. It was ordered that the church be closed, and that the perpetrators, after being subjected to a disciplinary punishment, be tried before a military tribunal.

*Berestechko, August 1920*

# SQUADRON COMMANDER TRUNOV

A T NOON WE BROUGHT the shot-through body of
Trunov, our squadron commander, to Sokal. He had
been killed that morning in battle with enemy aeroplanes.
Trunov had taken all the hits in his face—his cheeks were
studded with wounds, his tongue torn out. We washed the
dead man's face as best we could, so as to make its appearance
less terrible; we placed the Caucasian saddle at the head of
the coffin and dug Trunov a grave in a solemn place—in the
public garden, in the centre of town, near the cathedral. Our
squadron assembled on horseback, along with the regimental
staff and the division's military commissar. And at the stroke
of two on the cathedral clock, our decrepit little canon gave
the first shot. She saluted the dead commander with all of
her old three inches—she made a full salute, and we carried
the coffin to the open pit. The coffin's lid was open, and the
clean midday sun lit the long corpse, its mouth, stuffed with
broken teeth, and the polished boots, with their heels placed
together, as if on drill.

"Fighters," Pugachov, the regimental commander, said
then, gazing at the deceased and taking his place at the edge
of the pit. "Fighters," he said, trembling and stretching his

arms down his seams. "We're burying Pasha Trunov, a world hero, giving Pasha the final honour..."

And lifting his eyes, red-hot with sleeplessness, to the sky, Pugachov shouted out a speech about the dead fighters of the First Cavalry, about this proud phalanx pounding the anvil of future centuries with the hammer of history. Pugachov shouted his speech loudly. He clutched the hilt of his curved Chechen sabre and dug at the earth with his ragged, silver-spurred feet. After his speech the orchestra played the 'Internationale' and the Cossacks bid farewell to Pashka Trunov. The entire squadron jumped onto their horses and fired a volley into the air, our three-incher mumbled a second time, and we sent three Cossacks out for a wreath. They raced off, shooting at a full gallop, dropping out of their saddles and pulling fancy tricks, and they brought back whole armfuls of red flowers. Pugachov scattered these flowers beside the grave, and we stepped up to give Trunov a final kiss. I stood in the back ranks. I touched my lips to his brightened forehead, topped with a saddle, and walked off into town, into Gothic Sokal, which lay in dark-blue dust and indomitable Galician gloominess.

A large square stretched out to the left of the garden, a square built round with ancient synagogues. Jews in torn frock coats were quarrelling in the square, dragging each other about in incomprehensible blindness. Some of them—the Orthodox—praised the teachings of Hadas, the rebbe of Belz, and for this the Orthodox were attacked by Hasidim of the moderate persuasion, followers of the Husiatyn rebbe,

Judah. The Jews were arguing about the Kabbalah and made mention in their disputes of the name of Elijah, the Vilna Gaon,[1] the persecutor of the Hasidim…

"Elijah!" they'd shout, writhing and opening wide their hair-covered mouths.

Forgetting the war and the gun volleys, the Hasidim abused the very name of Elijah, the Vilna high priest, and I, pining with grief over Trunov, also jostled and bawled with them for my relief, until I saw before me a Galician as long and ghastly as Don Quixote.

This Galician was dressed in a white linen shirt that reached down to his toes. He was dressed as though for burial or for Communion, and he led a dishevelled little cow behind him on a rope. Atop his gigantic torso sat the mobile, shaved little head of a snake; it was covered with a wide-brimmed hat of village straw and teetered slightly. The pathetic little cow walked behind the Galician on his rein; he led it with an air of importance and cleaved the hot lustre of the heavens with the gallows of his long bones.

With solemn step he bypassed the square and entered a crooked lane steeped in thick, nauseating fumes. In the charred little houses, in the beggarly kitchens, Jewesses pottered about looking like old Negresses—Jewesses with exorbitant breasts. The Galician passed them by and stopped at the end of the lane before the pediment of a shattered building. There, near the pediment, near a warped white column, sat a Gypsy blacksmith shoeing horses. The Gypsy pounded the hooves with his hammer, shaking his greasy hair, whistling and smiling. A few Cossacks with horses stood around him. My Galician came up to the blacksmith, silently handed him a dozen baked potatoes and, without looking at anyone, turned back. I would have marched off after him, because I couldn't understand what kind of man he was and what kind of life he led here in Sokal, but I was stopped by a Cossack who was keeping his unshod horse at the ready. This Cossack's surname was Seliverstov. He'd left Makhno at some point and was now serving in the Thirty-Third Cavalry Regiment.

"Lyutov," he said, taking my hand in greeting. "You pick on everybody. There's a devil in you, Lyutov—why'd you have to go and cripple Trunov this morning?…"

And relying on foolish hearsay Seliverstov shouted some absolute nonsense at me, about how that morning I'd supposedly beaten up Trunov, my squadron commander. Seliverstov reproached me in every possible way for this, reproached me in front of all the Cossacks, but there wasn't a hint of truth in his story. Trunov and I had quarrelled that morning, it's true, because Trunov was always winding up an endless rigmarole with the prisoners; we'd quarrelled, but he died, Pashka, he has no more judges in this world, and I, of all people, am the last one to judge him. Here's why we fought.

We'd taken today's prisoners at dawn at the Zawada station. There were ten of them. They were in their underwear when we took them. A pile of clothes lay at the Poles' side; this was a ploy of theirs, so that we wouldn't be able to distinguish the officers from the rank and file by their uniforms. They'd thrown their clothes off themselves, but this time Trunov decided to get the truth.

"Officers, step forward!" he commanded as he approached the prisoners and pulled out his revolver.

Trunov had already been wounded in the head that morning. His head was bound with a rag, and blood dripped from it like rain from a hayrick.

"Officers, confess!" he repeated and began prodding the Poles with the butt of his revolver.

Then a lean old man stepped out from the crowd—a man with large bare bones on his back, yellow cheekbones and a drooping moustache.

"…War over," the old man said in broken Ukrainian with incomprehensible rapture. "All officers ran, war over…"

And the Pole stretched out his blue hands to the squadron commander.

"Five fingers," he said, sobbing and twirling his huge limp hand. "With these five fingers I reared my family…"

The old man choked, swayed, dissolved in rapturous tears and fell to his knees before Trunov, but Trunov pushed him away with his sabre.

"Your officers are scum," said the squadron commander. "Your officers went and threw their clothes off… If the clothes fit—that's the end of you. I'll make a trial…"

And then the squadron commander picked a cap with piping from the pile of rags and pulled it down over the old man's eyes.

"Just right," Trunov muttered, moving closer and whispering, "just right…" And he stuck his sabre into the prisoner's gullet. The old man fell, waggled his legs, and a frothy coral stream flowed from his throat. Then Andryushka Vosmiletov, glittering with his earring and round villager's neck, crept up to him. Andryushka undid the Pole's buttons, shook him gently and began pulling the trousers off the dying man. He threw them onto his saddle, took another two uniforms from the pile, and then rode away from us and started playing with his whip. At that moment the sun came out from behind the clouds. It swiftly surrounded Andryushka's horse, her joyous run, the carefree swaying of her docked tail. Andryushka was riding along the path to the woods; our unit transport was in the woods, and the transport's coachmen were having a devil of a good time, whistling and making signs at Vosmiletov as if he were a deaf-mute.

The Cossack was already halfway there, but then Trunov suddenly fell to his knees and rasped after him:

"Andrei," said the squadron commander, gazing at the ground. "Andrei," he repeated, without raising his eyes from the ground, "our Soviet republic is still alive—too soon to be carving it up. Drop those rags, Andrei."

But Vosmiletov didn't even turn around. He rode on at his astonishing Cossack trot, his little horse pertly tossing her tail out from under her, as if waving us away.

"Treason!" Trunov muttered, astonished. "Treason!" he said, quickly brought his carbine to his shoulder, fired, and missed in his hurry. But this time Andrei stopped. He turned his horse towards us and started jumping up and down in the saddle like a woman, his face red and angry and his legs jerking.

"Listen, countryman," he shouted, riding up, and immediately calmed down at the sound of his own deep and powerful voice. "I ought to knock you right into the next world, countryman... You clean up a dozen Poles—look what a fuss you make. We done cleaned up hundreds—never even called you... If you're a worker—do your work..."

Throwing the trousers and two uniforms from his saddle, Andrei snorted and turned away from the squadron commander. He undertook to help me compile a list of the remaining prisoners. He kept moving about, snorting extraordinarily loudly, and this bustling of his weighed heavily on me. The prisoners howled and ran from Andryushka; he chased after them, taking hold of them like a hunter takes hold of an armful of reeds so as to get a better view of a flock descending on a river at dawn.

Dealing with the prisoners I exhausted all my curses and managed to record eight men, along with their unit numbers and the kinds of weapon they carried, and moved on to the ninth. This ninth was a youth who looked like a German gymnast from a good circus—a youth with a proud German chest and sideburns, wearing a tricot jersey and a pair of Jäger drawers. He turned the two nipples on his high chest towards me, tossed back his sweaty white hair and named his unit. At that point Andrei grabbed him by the drawers and asked him sternly:

"Where'd you get the undies?"

"My ma knitted them," the prisoner answered and swayed.

"You've got a ma like a factory," Andrei said, peering at the drawers, and touched the Pole's manicured nails with the pads of his fingers. "A ma like a factory. Our boys've never sewn a thing like that…"

He felt the Jäger drawers again and then took the ninth by the arm, in order to lead him over to the rest of the prisoners who had already been recorded. But at that moment I saw Trunov crawling out from behind a mound. Blood dripped from the squadron commander's head like rain from a hayrick, his dirty rag had come loose and was hanging down, and he was crawling on his belly, holding his carbine in his hands. This was a Japanese carbine, lacquered and with a powerful charge. From a distance of twenty paces Pashka smashed the youth's skull and the Pole's brains spattered onto my hands. Then Trunov ejected the cartridge cases from the gun and walked over to me.

"Cross one out," he said, pointing to the list.

"I won't cross anything out," I said, shuddering. "It seems Trotsky's orders aren't meant for you, Pavel…"

"Cross one out!" Trunov repeated and jabbed the paper with a black finger.

"I won't cross anything out!" I shouted with all my strength. "There were ten, now there are eight—they won't even look at you at headquarters, Pashka…"

"At headquarters they'll look at it through this miserable life of ours," Trunov replied, and began moving towards me, all lacerated, hoarse and covered in smoke. But then he stopped, raised his bloodied head to the skies and said with bitter reproach: "Go on, keep on buzzing. There's another one buzzing…"

And the squadron commander showed us four points in the sky, four bombers sailing behind the shining, swan-like clouds. These were the planes of Major Fauntleroy's Air Escadrille—large armoured planes.[2]

"To horse!" the platoon commander shouted, catching sight of them, and led the squadron off to the woods at a trot, but Trunov did not ride with his squadron. He stayed at the station building, pressed himself against the wall and fell silent. Andryushka Vosmiletov and two machine-gunners, two barefoot fellows in crimson breeches, stood beside him, growing anxious.

"Bore the barrel, boys," Trunov told them, and blood began to drain from his face. "Here's my report to Pugachov…"

And on a crookedly torn piece of paper Trunov wrote, in gigantic peasant letters:

"*Having to die on this date*," he wrote, "*I consider it my duty to add two numbers to the potential downing of the enemy and at the same time hand over my command to Platoon Commander Semyon Golov…*"

He sealed the letter, sat down on the ground and, with a great effort, pulled off his boots.

"Use 'em," he said, handing the machine-gunners his report and the boots. "Use 'em, boots are new…"

"Good luck to you, Commander," the machine-gunners muttered in reply and shifted from foot to foot, hesitating to leave.

"And good luck to you," said Trunov. "One way or another, lads…" And he went over to the machine gun standing on the hillock by the station booth. Andryushka Vosmiletov, the ragman, was waiting for him there.

"One way or another," Trunov said to him, and started aiming the machine gun. "So you're sticking with me awhile, Andrei?…"

"Lord Jesus," Andryushka answered fearfully, sobbed, turned white and laughed. "Mother of Christ to the banners!…"

And he started aiming the second machine gun at the aeroplanes.

But the planes were flying ever more steeply over the station, rattling fussily up high, swooping down, describing circles, and the sun's rosy rays would land on the yellow lustre of their wings.

At that time we, the Fourth Squadron, were sitting in the woods. There, in the woods, we witnessed the unequal battle between Pashka Trunov and Major Reginald Fauntleroy of the American forces. The major and three of his bombardiers displayed considerable skill in this battle. They swooped down to three hundred metres and first strafed Andryushka, then Trunov. None of the cartridge belts that our men let loose caused the Americans any harm; they flew off without noticing the squadron hidden in the woods. And so, after waiting for half an hour, we were able to ride out and retrieve the corpses. Andryushka Vosmiletov's body was taken away by two of his kin, who were serving in our squadron, while the body of Trunov, our late commander, we brought to Gothic Sokal and buried him there in a solemn place, in a public garden, in a flowerbed, right in the middle of town.

# THE IVANS

**D**EACON AGEYEV had fled from the front twice. For this he'd been turned over to the Moscow "Branded" Regiment. Commander-in-Chief Sergei Sergeich Kamenev[1] was reviewing this regiment in Mozhaysk before sending it to its position.

"Don't need 'em," said the commander-in-chief. "Send 'em back to Moscow to clean latrines…"

In Moscow, they somehow knocked the branded together into an infantry company. The deacon wound up among them. He arrived at the Polish front and announced that he was deaf. After wasting a week on Ageyev, Medical Assistant Barsutsky of the first-aid detachment marvelled at his perseverance.

"To hell with 'im, the dum-dum," Barsutsky said to Soychenko, the medical orderly. "Go and get a cart from the transport—we'll send the deacon to Rovno for a test…"

Soychenko went to the transport and secured three carts. Akinfiyev was the coachman on the first one.

"Ivan," Soychenko said to him. "You'll take the dum-dum to Rovno."

"Can do," Akinfiyev replied.

"And you'll bring me back a receipt…"

"Understood," said Akinfiyev. "What's the cause of it, anyway—his deafness?…"

"Your own rug's worth more than some bastard's mug," said Soychenko, the medical orderly. "That's all the cause there is to it. He's no dum-dum, he's a faker…"

"Can do," repeated Akinfiyev, and rode off following the other carts.

Three carts drew up at the first-aid station. In the first one they put a nurse reassigned to the rear, the second was set aside for a Cossack suffering from nephritis, and Ivan Ageyev, the deacon, clambered up into the third.

Having seen to everything, Soychenko called the medical assistant.

"Our faker's on his way," he said. "I've loaded him on the Revolutionary Tribunal cart against a receipt. They're taking off now…"

Barsutsky glanced out of the little window, saw the carts and ran out of the house, all red in the face and hatless.

"You'll do him in!" he cried out to Akinfiyev. "We've got to move the deacon."

"Move 'im where?" some Cossacks standing nearby replied, and broke out laughing. "Wherever you put 'im, our Vanya's gonna get 'im…"

Akinfiyev was standing right there, beside his horses, with a whip in his hands. He took off his hat and said politely:

"Hello, Comrade Medical Assistant."

"Hello, friend," answered Barsutsky. "You know you're an animal—we've got to move the deacon…"

"I take an interest in knowing," the Cossack said shrilly, his upper lip twitching, creeping up and quivering above his dazzling teeth, "I take an interest in knowing if it's suitable for us or not suitable—when the enemy tyrannizes us unspeakably, when the enemy's knocking the wind out of us, when he hangs like a weight on our legs and wraps snakes around our arms—if it's suitable to plug your ears in this hour of mortal danger?"

"Vanya's standing up for the commissars," shouted Korotkov, the coachman from the first cart. "How he's standing up…"

"What do you mean, standing," Barsutsky muttered and turned away. "We're all standing. We've just got to do it properly…"

"Looks like he can hear fine, our dum-dum," Akinfiyev suddenly interrupted, twirled the whip in his thick fingers, laughed and winked at the deacon. Ageyev was sitting on the cart, his huge shoulders drooping, and moving his head.

"Well, take off, for God's sake!" the medic cried in despair. "You'll answer to me for everything, Ivan…"

"I'm willing to answer," Akinfiyev pronounced thoughtfully and bowed his head. "Get comfortable," he said to the deacon, without turning. "Get real comfortable," the Cossack repeated and gathered the reins in his hand.

The carts lined up in a row and raced off down the highway one after the other. Korotkov rode in front, and Akinfiyev was third. He was whistling a song and waving the reins. They covered about fifteen *verst*s, but towards evening were run off course by a sudden flood of enemy troops.

On that day, 22 July, the Poles mangled our army's rear with a rapid manoeuvre, swooped into the shtetl of Kozin and captured many fighters from the Eleventh Division. The Sixth Division's squadrons were flung to the area of Kozin so as to counter the enemy. The lightning-fast manoeuvring of the units chopped the transports to bits; the Revolutionary Tribunal carts wandered across the seething salients of battle for two days, and only on the third night did they find their way onto the road along which the rearguard staffs were retreating. It was on this road, at midnight, that I met them.

Numb with despair, I met them after the battle of Khotin. My horse was killed in the battle of Khotin—Lavrik, my comfort on this earth. After losing him I moved over to the ambulance wagon and picked up wounded men till evening. Then those who weren't wounded were kicked off the wagon, and I was left alone beside a ruined hut. Night flew towards me on swift steeds. The wail of the transports filled the universe. Roads were dying on an earth girdled with squeals. Stars crept out of the night's cool belly, and deserted villages flared up over the horizon. Shouldering my saddle, I set off along a ravaged boundary path and stopped at the bend to take a piss. Having relieved myself, I buttoned up and felt spray on my hands. I switched on my flashlight, turned around, and saw a Pole's corpse on the ground, bathed in my urine. It came spilling out of his mouth, sputtering between his teeth, pooling in his empty eye sockets. Beside the corpse lay a notebook and scraps of Piłsudski's proclamations. The Pole's notebook contained a record of his expenses, the schedule of performances at the Cracow Dramatic Theatre and the birthday of a woman named Maria Luiza. Using one of Marshal and Commander-in-Chief Piłsudski's proclamations, I wiped the stinking liquid from my unknown brother's skull and walked on, bent beneath the saddle's weight.

At that moment wheels groaned somewhere close by.

"Halt!" I cried, freezing in place. "Who's there?"

Night flew towards me on swift steeds, and fires writhed on the horizon.

"From the Revolutionary Tribunal," answered a voice smothered by darkness.

I ran forward and bumped into a cart.

"They killed my horse," I said, unusually loudly. "His name was Lavrik…"

No one answered. I climbed onto the cart, put the saddle under my head, fell asleep and slept until dawn, warmed by the musty hay and the body of Ivan Akinfiyev, my chance neighbour.

In the morning the Cossack woke up after me.

"Day's breaking, thank God," he said, then pulled a revolver from under his little trunk and fired a shot over the deacon's ear. The deacon was sitting right in front of us, driving the horses. Wispy grey hair fluttered above the bulk of his balding skull. Akinfiyev fired again over his other ear and slid the revolver back into its holster.

"Good morning, Vanya!" he said to the deacon, grunting and pulling on his boots. "Let's get some grub, eh?"

"Hold on," I cried, coming to my senses. "What're you doing?"

"Whatever I'm doing ain't enough," Akinfiyev replied, getting out the food. "He's been feigning with me for three days now…"

Then Korotkov, whom I knew from the Thirty-First Regiment, called back from the first cart and told the deacon's whole story from the start. Akinfiyev listened to him attentively, cupping his ear, then pulled a roast leg of ox from under a saddle. It was covered in sackcloth and had straw sticking to it. The deacon climbed over to us from the box, sliced the green meat with a little knife and handed each of us a piece. When breakfast was done, Akinfiyev tied the ox leg up in a bag and stuck it in the hay.

"Vanya," he said to Ageyev, "let's go chase out the devil. Gotta stop anyway, horses need water…"

He pulled a phial of medicine from his pocket along with a Tarnovsky syringe[2] and handed them to the deacon. They got down from the cart and walked about twenty yards into the field.

"Nurse," Korotkov cried out from the first cart, "fix your eyes into the distance—Akinfiyev's gifts are liable to strike you blind."

"Screw you, with your gifts," the woman muttered and turned away.

Akinfiyev then rolled up his shirt. The deacon got down

on his knees in front of him and did the syringing. Then
he wiped the syringe with a rag and held it up to the light.
Akinfiyev pulled up his trousers; seizing the moment, he
went behind the deacon's back and fired another shot right
over his ear.

"Much obliged, Vanya," he said, buttoning up.

The deacon put the phial down on the grass and rose
from his knees. His wispy hair flew up.

"A superior court will judge me," he said dully. "You're
not above me, Ivan…"

"Deeze days errybody judges errybody," interrupted the
driver from the second cart, who looked like an insolent
hunchback. "And condemn ya to death, just like dat…"

"Or better yet," Ageyev said and straightened up, "kill
me, Ivan…"

"Quit fooling around, Deacon," said Korotkov, whom
I knew from the old days, as he approached Ageyev.
"Understand what kind of man you're riding with. Another
man would've picked you off like a duck, wouldn't even quack,
but he's fishing the truth out of you and teaching you, you
unfrocked priest…"

"Or better yet," the deacon repeated stubbornly and
stepped forward, "kill me, Ivan."

"You'll kill yourself, bastard," replied Akinfiyev, turning
pale and lisping. "You'll dig your own pit, and you'll bury
yourself in it…"

He threw up his hands, tore his collar and fell to the
ground in a fit.

"My little drop of blood!" he shouted wildly and started pouring sand on his face. "My bitter little drop of blood, my Soviet power…"

"Vanya," Korotkov approached Akinfiyev and placed his hand tenderly on his shoulder. "Get a hold of yourself, dear friend, don't let it get to you. We've got to get going, Vanya…"

Korotkov took a mouthful of water and sprinkled it on Akinfiyev, then moved him over to the cart. The deacon sat on the box again and we drove off.

We had no more than two *verst*s to go before we reached the shtetl of Verba. Innumerable transports had huddled together in the shtetl that morning. The Eleventh Division was there, and the Fourteenth, and the Fourth. Jews in waistcoats, their shoulders hunched, stood at their thresholds like plucked birds. Cossacks were going from house to house, collecting towels and eating unripe plums. As soon as we arrived, Akinfiyev crawled into the hay and fell asleep, while I took a blanket from his cart and went to look for a place in the shade. But on both sides of the road the field was strewn with excrement. A bearded peasant in copper-rimmed glasses and a Tyrolean hat, who was reading a newspaper nearby, caught my gaze and said:

"Call ourselves men but foul things up worse than jackals. A shame to the earth…"

Turning away, he again began reading the newspaper through his big glasses.

I made for a small wood on the left and spotted the deacon, who was coming closer and closer.

"Where you rolling off to, countryman?" Korotkov shouted to him from the first cart.

"To relieve myself," muttered the deacon, then grabbed my hand and kissed it.

"You are a fine gentleman," he whispered, grimacing, shivering and gasping for breath. "I beg you, when you have a minute, write to the town of Kasimov, let my wife cry over me…"

"Are you deaf, Father Deacon," I shouted point-blank, "or not?"

"Pardon?" he said. "Pardon?" And he brought his ear closer.

"Are you deaf, Ageyev, or not?"

"Yes, that's right, deaf," he said quickly. "Two days ago I had perfect hearing, but Comrade Akinfiyev crippled my hearing with his shooting. He was supposed to deliver me to Rovno, Comrade Akinfiyev, but I don't believe he'll deliver me…"

And, falling to his knees, the deacon crawled between the carts head first, all tangled in dishevelled priestly hair. Then he rose from his knees, wriggled himself free from between the carts and walked over to Korotkov. The driver poured out some tobacco for him; they both rolled cigarettes and lit each other up.

"That's right," said Korotkov and cleared a space beside him. The deacon sat down next to him and they fell silent.

Then Akinfiyev woke up. He dumped the ox leg from the bag, sliced the green meat with a little knife and handed each of us a piece. On seeing this rotten leg I felt weakness and despair, and I handed back my meat.

"Goodbye, boys," I said. "Good luck to you…"

"Goodbye," replied Korotkov.

I took my saddle from the cart and walked off. Walking off, I heard the endless muttering of Ivan Akinfiyev.

"Vanya," he was saying to the deacon. "You've gone and stepped in it, Vanya. You should've been afraid of my name, but you've gone and sat in my cart. If you could still hop around before I got my hands on you, you won't be doing any hopping now. I'll give you a real good time, Vanya, a good time sure as hell…"

# THE STORY OF A HORSE, CONTINUED

FOUR MONTHS AGO Savitsky, our former division
commander, took a white stallion from Khlebnikov,
commander of the First Squadron. Khlebnikov then left the
army, but today Savitsky received a letter from him.

Khlebnikov to Savitsky:

> *And I can't hold any kind of grudge against Budyonny's army
> any more, and understand all my sufferings in that army and
> keep them in my heart, purer than a shrine. And to you, Comrade
> Savitsky, a worldwide hero, the toiling masses of Vitebsk, where
> I'm chairman of the Revolutionary Committee, send a proletarian
> cry—"Give us the world revolution!"—and hope that the white
> stallion walks under you for many years along soft trails, for the
> benefit of the freedom we all love and of the brotherly republics,
> where we ought to keep a special eye on the local authorities and
> district units in respect to administration…*

Savitsky to Khlebnikov:

> *My true Comrade Khlebnikov! That letter you wrote to me, it's
> very commendable for the common cause, especially, I'd say, after*

*that dumb thing you did, when you draped your own selfish hide over your eyes and marched out of our Communist Party of Bolsheviks. Our Communist Party, Comrade Khlebnikov, is an iron column of fighters, who give their blood in the front rank, and when blood flows from iron, Comrade, it's no joke—it's victory or death. The same goes for the common cause, which I don't expect I'll see dawning, because the fighting is heavy and I'm changing command staff every two weeks. Thirty days now I've been fighting in the rearguard, covering the invincible First Cavalry under the enemy's effective rifle, artillery and aeroplane fire. Tardy's dead, Lukhmanikov's dead, Lykoshenko's dead, Gulevoy's dead, Trunov's dead, and there's no white stallion under me, so, in accordance with a change in the fortunes of war, don't expect to see your beloved Division Commander Savitsky, Comrade Khlebnikov—we'll see each other, to put it plainly, in the kingdom of heaven, but I hear the old man isn't running a kingdom up there, he's running a proper whorehouse, and there's enough clap here on earth, so maybe we won't be seeing each other. Farewell, Comrade Khlebnikov.*

*Galicia, September 1920*

# THE WIDOW

Shevelyov, the regimental commander, lies dying on an ambulance cart. A woman sits at his feet. Night, pierced by a cannonade's flashes, arches over the dying man. Lyovka, the division commander's coachman, is warming up food in a pot. Lyovka's forelock hangs over the fire; the hobbled horses crunch in the bushes. Lyovka stirs the pot with a twig, saying to Shevelyov, who's stretched out on the ambulance cart:

"I worked, dear comrade, in the town of Temryuk—worked as a trick rider, and as a lightweight athlete too. Little town's a bore for a woman, of course—ladies caught sight of me, started tearing down the walls… 'Lev Gavrilych, you won't refuse a snack à la carte, will you? You won't regret the time you lose…' So I go off to a tavern with one of 'em. We order two portions of veal, order a jug, and we sit there nice and quiet, drinking… I look around—some kind of gentleman's making his way towards me, dressed not so bad, neat, but I notice he's got a lot of imagination to 'im, and he ain't on his first drink…

"'Excuse me,' he says. 'What, by the way, is your nationality?'

"'What reason have you got, mister, to touch me on nationality,' I ask, 'especially when I'm in the ladies' society?'

"And he:

"'You're no athlete,' he says. 'In French wrestling, they knock your kind flat. Prove your nation…'

"But I'm telling you, I still didn't get it.

"'Why'd you, and I don't know your proper name,' I say, 'why'd you have to go and provoke such a misunderstanding, so that now someone's got to die right here, in other words, lie down to the last breath?' To the last…" Lyovka repeats ecstatically and stretches his arms to the sky, gathering the night about him like a halo.

The tireless wind, the clean wind of night, sings, filled with ringing, gently rocking the soul. Stars blaze in the dark like wedding rings; they fall on Lyovka, get tangled in his hair and fade in his shaggy head.

"Lev," Shevelyov suddenly whispers to him through blue lips, "come here. Whatever gold I've got—goes to Sashka," says the wounded man. "The rings, the harness—all goes to her. We lived as best we could… I'll reward her. My clothes, underwear, medal for selfless heroism—to my mother on the Terek. Send it with a letter and write in the letter—with regards from the commander, and don't cry. The hut's yours, old woman—live. Anyone bothers you, gallop right off to Budyonny: I'm Shevelyov's ma. My steed Abramka, I give it up to the regiment, give it up to cover the expenses…"

"I'll see they get the steed," Lyovka mutters and waves his hands. "Sash," he shouts to the woman, "heard what he said?... Declare right in front of 'im—you gonna give the old woman what's hers or not?..."

"To hell with your mother," Sashka answers and walks off into the bushes, her back straight as a blind man's.

"Gonna give up the orphan's share?" Lyovka catches up to her and grabs her by the throat. "Say it in front of 'im..."

"I'll give it up. Let go of me."

Having forced the declaration, Lyovka took the pot from the fire and began pouring the *shchi* into the dying man's stiffened mouth. The cabbage soup trickled down from Shevelyov, the spoon rattled against his gleaming dead teeth and the bullets sang ever louder, ever more dreary in the dense expanses of night.

"Hitting us with rifles, the snakes," said Lyovka.

"Aristo lackeys," replied Shevelyov. "Cutting us open on the right flank with machine guns..."

And closing his eyes, all solemn, like a corpse on a table, Shevelyov commenced listening to the battle with his large, waxen ears. Lyovka was chewing meat beside him, crunching and panting. When he was finished with the meat, Lyovka licked his lips and dragged Sashka into a hollow.

"Sash," he said, trembling, belching and wringing his hands. "Sash, we're all sinners in God's eyes anyway... Live once, die once. Give in, Sash—I'll pay you back in blood, if I have to... His time's come and gone, Sash, but God's days ain't running out..."

They sat down on the tall grass. The sluggish moon crept

out from behind the clouds and lingered on Sashka's bare knee.

"You're getting warm," muttered Shevelyov, "but it looks like they've routed the Fourteenth Division…"

Lyovka crunched and panted in the bushes. The hazy moon drifted across the sky like a beggar woman. Distant gunfire floated in the air. Feather grass rustled on the troubled earth, and August stars fell into the grass.

Then Sashka returned to her previous place. She started to change the wounded man's bandages and raised the flashlight over the rotting wound.

"You'll be gone by tomorrow," Sashka said, wiping Shevelyov, who was sweating a cold sweat. "Gone by tomorrow, it's in your guts, death…"

And at that moment a tight, vociferous blow crashed into the earth. Four fresh brigades, led into battle by the enemy's unified command, fired the first shell over Busk, severing our communications and lighting up the Bug watershed. Obedient fires rose on the horizon; the weighty birds of a cannonade flew up from the flames. Busk burnt, and Lyovka, the stunned lackey, flew through the woods in the Sixth Division commander's reeling carriage. He pulled at the scarlet reins, striking the lacquered wheels against tree stumps. Shevelyov's cart raced after him with the attentive Sashka guiding the horses, which were straining at their harnesses.

That's how they came to the first-aid station at the edge of the woods. Lyovka unharnessed the horses and went to the officer in charge to ask for a horse blanket. He walked through the woods, which were cluttered with carts. The bodies of medical orderlies stuck out from under the carts, and a timid dawn fought through soldiers' sheepskins. The sleeping men's boots were thrust apart, their pupils turned to the sky, the black pits of their mouths twisted.

The officer had a blanket; Lyovka returned to Shevelyov, kissed his forehead and drew the blanket over his head. Then Sashka approached the cart. She'd tied her kerchief under her chin and shaken the straw from her dress.

"Pavlik," she said. "My Jesus Christ." And she lay down sideways on the dead man, covering him with her immense body.

"Grieving," Lyovka said then. "No denying it, they had a good life. Now she'll be under the whole squadron again. Tough…"

And he rode on to Busk, where the staff of the Sixth Cavalry Division had set itself up.

There, about ten *versts* from town, we were engaging the Savinkov Cossacks.[1] The traitors fought under the command of Cossack Captain Yakovlev, who'd gone over to the Poles. They fought bravely. For the second day in a row, the division commander was out with the troops; not finding him at headquarters, Lyovka returned to his hut, brushed the horses, doused the carriage wheels with water and lay down to sleep in the threshing barn. The barn was full of fresh hay, as incendiary as perfume. Lyovka had a good sleep and then sat down to dinner. His hostess boiled him some potatoes and poured sour clotted milk over them. Lyovka was already sitting at the table when the funereal wail of trumpets and the tramping of many hooves sounded in the street. The squadron, with its trumpeters and standards, was moving along the winding Galician street. Shevelyov's body lay on a gun carriage, covered with banners. Sashka rode behind the coffin on Shevelyov's stallion; a Cossack song oozed from the ranks at the rear.

The squadron passed along the main street and turned towards the river. Then Lyovka, barefoot and capless, set off running after the retreating detachment and grabbed the reins of the squadron commander's horse.

Neither the division commander, who'd stopped at the crossroads and saluted the dead commander, nor his staff could hear what Lyovka said to the squadron commander.

"…Underwear…" The wind brought us snatches of words. "…Mother on the Terek…" We heard Lyovka's incoherent cries. Without hearing him out to the end, the squadron commander freed his reins and pointed to Sashka. The woman shook her head and rode on. Lyovka then jumped into her saddle, grabbed her hair, bent back her head and smashed her face with his fist. Sashka wiped the blood away with the hem of her skirt and rode on. Lyovka climbed down from the saddle, tossed back his forelock and tied a red scarf around his hips. And the howling trumpeters led the squadron on to the gleaming line of the Bug.

Soon he returned to us, Lyovka, the division commander's lackey, and shouted, his eyes flashing:

"I gave it to her good… I'll send it to the mother, she says, when time comes. I'll keep his memory, she says, I'll remember myself. If you remember, you snake, then don't you forget… And if you forget—we'll remind you. Forget a second time—we'll remind you a second time…"

*Galicia, August 1920*

# ZAMOŚĆ

T HE DIVISION COMMANDER and his staff lay on a mowed field about three *verst*s from Zamość. The troops were to launch a night assault on the town. We'd been ordered to spend the night in Zamość, and the division commander was awaiting reports of victory.

It was raining. Wind and darkness raced over the drenched earth. The stars had all been stifled by the spreading ink of the clouds. Exhausted horses sighed and shifted from foot to foot in the murk. We had nothing to give them. I tied my horse's reins to my leg, wrapped myself up in my cloak and lay down in a pit full of water. The sodden earth offered me the soothing embrace of the grave. The horse drew her reins and pulled at my leg. She'd found a tuft of grass and began nibbling at it. Then I fell asleep and dreamt of a barn strewn with hay. The dusty gold of threshing hummed above the barn. Sheaves of wheat flew across the sky, the July day was passing into evening and thickets of sunset were thrown back over the village.

I was stretched out on a silent bed, and the tender caress of hay at the nape of my neck was driving me mad. Then the barn doors parted with a whine. A woman dressed for a ball approached me. She freed her chest from the black lace of her bodice and brought it towards me with care, like a wet nurse. She placed her chest against mine. The agonizing heat shook the very foundations of my soul, and droplets of sweat—living, moving sweat—came to a boil between our nipples.

"Margot," I wanted to cry out, "the earth is dragging me along on the cord of its calamities, like a jibbing dog, but still I managed to see you, Margot…"

I wanted to cry this out, but my jaws, seized shut by a sudden chill, would not unclench. Then the woman pulled away from me and fell to her knees.

"Jesus," she said, "receive the soul of thy departed servant…"

She fixed two worn five-copeck pieces onto my eyelids and stuffed the opening of my mouth with sweet-smelling hay. A cry circled my shackled jaws in vain, my dimming pupils turned slowly beneath the copper coins, I couldn't unclasp my hands and… I awoke.

A peasant with a matted beard lay in front me. He had a rifle in his hands. My horse's back cleaved the sky like a black crossbar. My leg was stuck up in the air, gripped by the tight noose of the reins.

"Fell asleep, countryman," the peasant said and smiled with his sleepless, night-time eyes. "Horse hauled you half a *verst*…"

I untied the strap and stood up. Blood was dripping down my face, lacerated by weeds.

There, just a couple of paces away, lay the front line. I could see the chimneys of Zamość, the furtive lights in the ravines of its ghetto and the watchtower with its broken lantern. The damp dawn came washing over us like waves of chloroform. Green rockets soared above the Polish camp. They'd flutter in the air, come apart like roses shedding petals beneath the moon and fade away.

And in the stillness I heard the distant breath of a groan. The smoke of secret murder wandered around us.

"They're killing somebody," I said. "Who're they killing?…"

"Pole's getting worked up," the peasant replied. "Pole's cutting down Jews…"

The peasant shifted the rifle from his right hand to his left. His beard was bent entirely to one side. He looked at me with affection and said:

"Nights are long on the line—no end to these nights. And a man gets so he wants to talk to another man, but where's he gonna find another man round here?…"

The peasant made me light my cigarette from his.

"Jew's guilty in everyone's eyes," he said, "yourn and ourn. There'll be mighty few of 'em left after the war. How many Jews are there in the world, anyway?"

"Ten million," I answered, and began to bridle my horse.

"There'll be two hundred thousand left," the peasant cried out and touched my hand, afraid that I would leave. But I climbed into the saddle and galloped off towards the staff.

The division commander was already preparing to ride off. Orderlies stood to attention in front of him, sleeping as they stood. Dismounted squadrons crawled over wet hillocks.

"They're putting the screws on us," the division commander whispered and rode off.

We followed him along the road to Sitaniec.

The rain started again. Dead mice floated down the roads. Autumn laid an ambush around our hearts, and trees—naked corpses set upright on both feet—swayed at the crossroads.

We arrived in Sitaniec in the morning. I was with Volkov, the staff quartermaster. He found us a free hut at the edge of the village.

"Vodka," I said to the hostess. "Vodka, meat and bread!"

The old woman was sitting on the floor, hand-feeding a calf hidden under the bed.

"*Nic nie ma*,"[1] she replied indifferently. "Can't remember the last time there was anything…"

I sat down at the table, took off my revolver and fell asleep. A quarter of an hour later I opened my eyes and saw Volkov, hunched over the window sill. He was writing a letter to his bride.

"*My dear Valya*," he wrote, "*do you remember me?*"

I read the first line, then took matches from my pocket and set fire to a pile of straw on the floor. The freed flame blazed up and rushed towards me. The old woman lay down with her chest on the fire and put it out.

"What are you doing, Pan?" the old woman said, retreating in horror.

Volkov turned, fixed the hostess with his vacant eyes and then went back to his letter.

"I'm gonna burn you down, hag," I muttered, falling asleep, "burn you down with your stolen calf."

"*Czekaj!*"[2] the hostess shouted in a high voice. She ran out into the entryway and came back with a jug of milk and some bread.

We didn't have time to eat half of it before shots broke out, rattling in the yard. There were a lot of them. They kept on rattling for a long time, getting on our nerves. We finished the milk and Volkov went out into the yard to see what was going on.

"I saddled your horse," he told me through the little window. "They riddled mine. The Poles are setting up machine guns a hundred paces off."

And so we had one horse left for the both of us. She barely carried us out of Sitaniec. I sat in the saddle and Volkov huddled up behind me.

The transports were fleeing, roaring, sinking in the mud. Morning came oozing down on us like chloroform oozing down on a hospital table.

"Are you married, Lyutov?" Volkov said suddenly, sitting behind me.

"My wife left me," I answered, then dozed off for a few moments and dreamt I was sleeping in a bed.

Silence.

Our horse staggers.

"Mare's gonna give out in a couple of *verst*s," says Volkov, sitting behind me.

Silence.

"Lost the campaign," mutters Volkov, and gives a snort.

"Yes," I say.

*Sokal, September 1920*

# TREASON

"COMRADE INVESTIGATOR BURDENKO. I write in response to your question that I've got myself a Partisanship, number twenty-four double zero, issued to Nikita Balmashov by the Krasnodar Party Committee. I explain my biography prior to 1914 as a domestic one, wherein I tilled the soil with my parents and then transferred from tilling to the ranks of the imperialists, so as to defend Citizen Poincaré and the hangman of the German revolution, Ebert-Noske, who must've been sleeping and seeing in their dreams how to lend a hand to my native Cossack village, Ivan Svyatoy in the Kuban province. And that's how the thread spun along until Comrade Lenin, together with Comrade Trotsky, turned my ferocious bayonet to the guts it was meant for, to a nicer belly. From that time on I wear the number twenty-four double zero on the end of my clear-sighted bayonet, and it's pretty shameful and just too funny for me to hear this rotten hogwash about some unknown N—— Hospital from you, Comrade Investigator Burdenko. I could give two shits about this hospital, but I didn't attack it or take any shots at it, and I couldn't have, anyway. Being wounded, the three of us, namely the fighters

Golovitsyn and Kustov and I, had a fever in the bones and didn't do any attacking, we just cried in our hospital gowns out in the square amid the free population, Jews by nationality. And concerning the damage to the three window panes, which we damaged with an officer's revolver, I tell you with all my heart that these window panes weren't serving their purpose, as they were in the storeroom, which didn't need them. And Dr Jawein, seeing this bitter shooting of ours, only sneered with all kinds of smirks, standing there in the window of his hospital, which can also be confirmed by the above-mentioned free Jews of the town of Kozin. As to this Dr Jawein, Comrade Investigator, I'll also submit the following material: he sneered at us wounded men, namely the fighters Golovitsyn and Kustov and me, when we originally enlisted for treatment, and from his first words spoke far too rough, saying, you fighters, go and wash up in the bathroom, each of you, and drop your weapons and your clothes this minute, I'm afraid of contagion, I'm sending them to the arsenal, no doubt about it... And then fighter Kustov, seeing a beast in front of him instead of a man, stepped forward with his broken leg and expressed himself, asking what kind of contagion could there be in a sharp Kuban sabre, except when it comes to the enemies of our revolution, and was also interested to learn about the arsenal, whether there was a Party fighter in there watching over things or, on the contrary, someone from the non-Party masses. And here Dr Jawein evidently saw that we understood treason well enough. He turned his back to us and, without another word, sent us off to the ward, and again with all kinds of smirks, and that's where we went, hobbling on our broken legs, waving our crippled arms and holding on to one another, as the three of us are countrymen from the Cossack village of Ivan Svyatoy, namely Comrades Golovitsyn and Kustov and I, we're all countrymen with one fate, and whoever's got a torn-up leg holds on to a comrade's arm, and whoever's missing an arm leans on a comrade's shoulder. In accordance with the issued order, we went to the ward, where we expected to see cultural-educational work and dedication to the cause, but what, it may interest you to know, did we see in that ward? We saw Red Army men, all infantry, sitting on covered beds and playing checkers, and tall nurses, plenty smooth, standing at the windows and handing out sympathy. We saw all this and froze in place, as if struck by thunder.

"'Done fighting, boys?' I exclaim to the wounded men.

"'Done,' the wounded men answer and move their checkers made of bread.

"'Too soon,' I say to the wounded men. 'Done too soon, infantry, when the enemy's prowling on soft paws fifteen *verst*s from town, and when you can read about our international situation in *The Red Cavalryman* newspaper, read that it's plain hell, and that the horizon's full of clouds.' But my words bounced off the heroic infantry like sheep dung off a regimental drum, and instead of a proper conversation, the merciful sisters led us off to bed and started droning on again about us surrendering our weapons, as if we'd already been defeated. Well, they got Kustov all stirred up, and he started picking at the wound on his left shoulder, right over the bloody heart of a fighter and proletarian. Seeing him straining like that, the nurses quieted down, but they only quieted down for the littlest while, and then they started up with their mockery again like the non-Party masses they were, and they'd send volunteers to pull our clothes out from under us as we slept, or they'd force us to play theatrical roles for cultural-educational work in women's dress, which isn't befitting.

"Merciless nurses. They made more than one attempt at us with sleeping powders, on account of the clothes, so we took to resting in turn, keeping one eye open, and we'd go to the latrine in full uniform, with revolvers, even to urinate. And after suffering like this for a week and a day, we started raving, getting visions, and then, when we woke up on the accursed morning of 4 August, we noticed that a change had taken place, that we were lying there in numbered robes, like convicts, without weapons and without the clothes woven by our mothers, feeble old women from the Kuban… And the sun, we see, is shining real fine, and the trench infantry, that had three Red Cavalrymen suffering in its midst, is riding roughshod all over us, and the merciless nurses, who poured us sleeping powders the night before, are shaking their young breasts, bringing us cocoa on plates, and there's enough milk in this cocoa to drown us! It was a regular merry carousel, with the infantry knocking around on their crutches loud as hell and pinching our sides like we was whores, bought and paid for, and saying she was done fighting too, Budyonny's

First Cavalry Army. But no, my curly-headed comrades, who grew yourselves some beautiful bellies that go off in the night like machine guns, she wasn't done fighting. No, the three of us made like we needed to go, and then we came out into the yard, where we set off in a fever, with our blue wounds, to Citizen Boyderman, chairman of the District Revolutionary Committee, and if it wasn't for him, Comrade Investigator Burdenko, this misunderstanding with the shooting might never even have happened, that is, if it wasn't for the chairman of the District Revolutionary Committee, who made us lose our minds altogether. And though we can't submit any solid material on Citizen Boyderman, it's just that when we walked in to meet with the chairman of the District Revolutionary Committee we saw a citizen of mature years in a sheepskin coat, a Jew by nationality, sitting at a desk, the desk so full of papers it's ugly to look at… Citizen Boyderman looks this way and that, and it's plain to see he can't understand a thing in these papers, he's miserable with these papers, especially since unknown but deserving fighters keep approaching Citizen Boyderman for rations in a threatening manner, and local workers shout over them to report on counter-revolutionaries in the surrounding villages, and then ordinary workers from the Centre show up, demanding to get married in the District Revolutionary Committee straight away and without any red tape… And we too raised our voices and presented the case of treason at the hospital, but Citizen Boyderman just goggled at us, looked this way and that, and caressed our shoulders, which is no longer authority and isn't worthy of authority. He wouldn't issue a resolution for the life of him, and only said: comrade fighters, if you pity Soviet authority, then leave these premises, to which we couldn't agree, that is, to leave the premises, and demanded his general identity card, upon not receiving which, we lost consciousness. And being without consciousness we went out into the square in front of the hospital, where we disarmed the militia consisting of one cavalryman and, with tears in our eyes, violated the three unenviable window panes in the above-described storeroom. Dr Jawein made faces and sneered at this intolerable fact, and this at a moment when Comrade Kustov was going to die of his illness in four days!

"In his short Red life, Comrade Kustov worried no end about treason, and there it is, winking at us from the window, there it is, sneering at the crude proletariat, but comrades, the proletariat himself knows he's crude, and it pains us, our soul burns and rends with fire the prison of our body and the jail of our hateful ribs…

"I tell you, Comrade Investigator Burdenko, treason laughs at us from the window, treason walks barefoot in our house, treason's tossed its boots over its shoulder, so that the floorboards don't creak in the house it's looting…"

# CZEŚNIKI

THE SIXTH DIVISION was mustered in the woods outside the village of Cześniki, waiting for the signal to attack. But Pavlichenko, the division commander, was awaiting the arrival of the Second Brigade and wouldn't give the signal. Then Voroshilov rode up to the division commander. He nudged him in the chest with his horse's muzzle and said:

"Wasting time, Division Commander, wasting time."

"The Second Brigade," Pavlichenko replied dully, "is moving to the scene of the action at a trot, in accordance with your orders."

"Wasting time, Division Commander, wasting time," said Voroshilov and pulled at his straps. Pavlichenko took a step back.

"In the name of conscience," he cried, and began wringing his clammy fingers, "in the name of conscience, don't rush me, Comrade Voroshilov…"

"Don't rush him," whispered Klim Voroshilov, member of the Revolutionary Military Council, and closed his eyes. He sat on his horse with his eyes closed, silent, moving his lips. A Cossack in bast shoes and a bowler hat gazed at him in bewilderment. The Army staff—strapping general staffers in

pants redder than human blood—did callisthenics behind his back and exchanged smiles. The galloping squadrons howled through the woods as the wind howls, breaking branches. Voroshilov combed his horse's mane with his Mauser.

"Army Commander," he shouted, turning to Budyonny, "say a few parting words to the troops. There he is, the Pole, standing on the hill just like a picture, laughing at you…"

And it's true—you could see the Poles through field glasses. The Army staff jumped onto their horses and the Cossacks flocked to them from all sides.

Ivan Akinfiyev, ex-wagoner for the Revolutionary Tribunal, rode past and nudged me with his stirrup.

"You at the front, Ivan?" I said to him. "But you haven't got any ribs…"

"Fuck ribs…" said Akinfiyev, who was sitting on his horse sideways. "Lemme 'ear what the man's got to say."

He rode forward and pressed right up against Budyonny.

Budyonny shuddered and said quietly:

"Boys, we've got a bad situation on our hands—got to liven it up, boys…"

"Give us Warsaw!" cried the Cossack in the bast shoes and bowler hat, opened his eyes wide and cut the air with his sabre.

"Give us Warsaw!" cried Voroshilov, reared his horse up and bolted into the midst of the squadrons.

"Men and commanders!" he said with passion. "In Moscow, in the ancient capital, an unprecedented power is waging battle. A government of workers and peasants, the first in the world, orders you, men and commanders, to attack the enemy and bring home victory."

"Sabres at the ready..." Pavlichenko sang out remotely behind the Army commander's back, and his foaming, turned-out crimson lips glistened in the ranks. The division commander's red Cossack coat was in tatters, his fleshy, hateful face contorted. He saluted Voroshilov with the blade of his priceless sabre.

"In accordance with my duty to the Revolutionary Oath," said the Sixth Division commander, wheezing and looking around, "I report to the Revolutionary Military Council of the First Cavalry: the Second Invincible Cavalry Brigade is approaching the scene of action at a trot."

"Get on with it," said Voroshilov and waved his arm. He touched the reins and Budyonny rode off beside him. They rode side by side on chestnut mares, wearing identical tunics and shining trousers embroidered with silver. The fighting men moved along behind them, raising a whoop, and pale steel shimmered in the ichor of the autumn sun. But I heard no unanimity in the Cossacks' whoop; awaiting the attack, I walked off into the woods, deep into the woods, to the first-aid and meal station.

Two plump nurses in aprons were lying there on the grass. They were nudging each other with their young breasts and pushing each other away. They were laughing the swooning laughter of women and winking at me from below, without blinking. That's how village girls wink at a parched lad— village girls with bare feet, who squeal like fondled puppies and spend their nights out in the yard, on the agonizing pillows of a hayrick. Farther on from the nurses a wounded Red Army man lay in delirium, and Styopka Duplishchev, a quarrelsome little Cossack, was curry-combing Hurricane, the thoroughbred stallion that belonged to the division commander and had been dammed by Lyulyusha, a prize-winner from Rostov. The wounded soldier was raving, recalling the town of Shuya, a heifer, some flax tow, while Duplishchev, drowning out the man's pathetic muttering, sang a song about an orderly and a fat general's wife, singing louder and louder, waving the curry comb up in the air and stroking the horse. But Sashka interrupted him—swollen Sashka, lady of all the squadrons. She rode up to the boy and jumped to the ground.

"C'mon, let's do it," Sashka said.

"Shove off," Duplishchev answered, turned his back to her and started braiding ribbons into Hurricane's mane.

"You speaking for yourself, Styopka?" Sashka said then. "Or you just putty?"

"Shove off," Styopka answered. "I'm speaking for myself."

He braided all the ribbons into the mane and suddenly cried out to me in despair:

"Just look here a minute, Kirill Vasilich, see how she hounds me? The whole month I been putting up with all kinds of things from 'er, can't even tell you what. Don't matter where I turn—there she is. Don't matter where I go—she's a fence on my path. It's let 'er have the stallion, let 'er have the stallion. Sure I will, when the division commander's telling me every day, Styopka, he says, with a stallion like that, you'll get lots of folks asking, but don't you let 'im go till he's in his fourth year…"

"Bet they let you go in your fifteenth," Sashka muttered and turned away. "In your fifteenth, I bet, and nothing came of it, you're all quiet, just blowing bubbles…"

She walked over to her mare, tightened the saddle-girths and got ready to ride. The spurs on her shoes jangled, her fishnet stockings were spattered with mud and trimmed with straw, and her monstrous breasts went swinging around to her back.

"Brought a rouble," Sashka said, looking off to the side, and placed her spurred shoe into the stirrup. "Brought one, and now I gotta take it back."

The woman took out two brand-new fifty-copeck pieces, played with them on her palm and slipped them back into her bosom.

"C'mon, let's do it," Duplishchev said then, without taking his eyes off the silver, and led up the stallion. Sashka chose a sloping place on the meadow and halted her mare.

"Seems you're the only one round here with a stallion," she said to Styopka, and started directing Hurricane. "It's just that my little mare's a frontline horse, hasn't had anyone over her in two years, so I think to myself, might as well get some good blood…"

Sashka handled the stallion and then led her horse off to the side:

"Now we've got our stuffing, girl," she whispered, and kissed the mare on her wet, piebald horse lips, with their dangling strands of spittle, rubbed up against the horse's muzzle, and then listened close to the noise stamping through the woods.

"The Second Brigade's coming," Sashka said sternly, and then turned to me. "We gotta ride, Lyutych…"

"Coming or not," Duplishchev cried out, and a spasm seized his throat, "you gotta pony up for what you got…"

"Money's right here," Sashka muttered and jumped onto the mare.

I raced after her and we moved off at a gallop. Duplischev's howl rang out behind us, along with the light rap of a gunshot.

"Just look here a minute!" the little Cossack cried, running through the woods just as fast as he could.

The wind leapt between the branches like a hare gone mad, the Second Brigade flew through the Galician oaks, and the serene dust of a cannonade rose above the ground as over a peaceful hut. And at a sign from the division commander we went on the attack, the unforgettable attack at Cześniki.

# AFTER THE BATTLE

T HE STORY OF MY FEUD with Akinfiyev goes like
this:

The attack at Cześniki took place on the 31st. Our squadrons amassed in the woods near the village and at five o'clock
in the evening rushed at the enemy. He was waiting for us
up on high ground, three *verst*s away. We covered the three
*verst*s on our infinitely weary horses and, leaping up on the
hill, met a lifeless wall of black uniforms and pallid faces.
These were Cossacks who'd betrayed us at the start of the
Polish battles and been gathered into a brigade by Cossack
Captain Yakovlev. Having formed the horseman into a
square, the captain was waiting for us with sabre drawn. A
gold tooth glistened in his mouth, and his black beard lay on
his chest like an icon on a corpse. The adversary's machine
guns were firing at twenty paces; men fell wounded in our
ranks. We trampled them and struck at the enemy, but its
square didn't falter—then we fled.

That's how Savinkov's men gained a short-lived victory
over the Sixth Division. It was gained because the object
under attack did not turn its face from the lava of our
onrushing squadrons. The captain stood fast this time, and we

fled without staining our swords crimson with the wretched blood of traitors.

Five thousand men, our whole division, came scudding down the slopes, with no one pursuing us. The enemy remained on the hill. He couldn't believe his improbable victory and didn't dare chase us. This is why we survived and slid down unharmed into the valley, where we were met by Vinogradov, head of the Sixth Division's political section. Vinogradov was charging about on a rabid steed, sending fleeing Cossacks back into battle.

"Lyutov," he cried, catching sight of me, "turn those fighters around, or it's the end of you…"

Vinogradov was belting his reeling stallion with the butt of his Mauser, screeching and gathering up men. I got away from him and rode over to Gulimov, the Kyrgyz, who was galloping close by:

"Turn your horse around, Gulimov," I said, "get up there…"

"Get up a mare's rear," answered Gulimov and glanced back. He glanced back furtively, fired a shot, and singed the hair above my ear.

"Turn yours back," Gulimov whispered, grabbed me round the shoulders, and tried to pull his sabre out with the other hand. The sabre sat tight in its scabbard. The Kyrgyz kept trembling, looking around. He held me by the shoulder, bending his face closer and closer to mine.

"Yours goes first," he repeated almost inaudibly, "mine goes behind"—and he struck me lightly in the chest with the

blade of his sabre, which had given way. The proximity of
death, its suffocating closeness, made me nauseous; I pressed
my palm against the Kyrgyz's face, which was as hot a stone
in the sun, and scratched him as deeply as I could. Warm
blood stirred beneath my fingernails, tickling them, and I
rode away from Gulimov, gasping for breath as after a long
journey. My tormented friend, my horse, moved slowly, at a
walk. I rode without seeing the way, rode without turning,
until I met Vorobyov, commander of the First Squadron.
Vorobyov was looking for his quartermasters, with no luck.
He and I came to the village of Cześniki and sat down on
a bench with Akinfiyev, ex-wagoner for the Revolutionary
Tribunal. Sashka, nurse of the Thirty-First Cavalry Regiment,
came walking past, and two commanders sat down next to us.
These commanders dozed silently; one of them, shell-shocked,
kept shaking his head uncontrollably and winking his bulging
eye. Sashka went off to report on him at the hospital and
then came back to us, dragging her horse by the reins. Her
mare was putting up a fight, its legs slipping in the wet clay.

"Where you setting sail for?" Vorobyov said to the nurse.
"Come and sit with us, Sash…"

"I won't," Sashka said, and hit her mare on the belly.
"Won't sit with you…"

"Why's that?" Vorobyov shouted, laughing. "Gone and
changed your mind about drinking tea with men, Sash?…"

"Changed my mind about you," the woman turned to the
commander and flung the reins away from herself. "Changed
my mind, Vorobyov, about drinking tea with you, 'cause I

seen you today, all you heroes, and you sure weren't pretty, Commander..."

"And when you seen it," muttered Vorobyov, "shoulda started shooting..."

"Shooting," Sashka said in despair and tore the hospital band from her sleeve. "I'm supposed to shoot with this, eh?"

That's when Akinfiyev, ex-wagoner for the Revolutionary Tribunal, with whom I had an old score to settle, moved up to us.

"You got nothing to shoot with, Sashok," he said, soothingly. "Nobody's faulting you there—who I'm faulting is folks that get all turned around when the fight's on, and don't load no cartridges in their guns... You went on the attack," Akinfiyev suddenly shouted at me, and a spasm took hold of his face. "You went but you didn't load no cartridges... Where's the reason for that?"

"Leave me be, Ivan," I said to Akinfiyev, but he wouldn't step back. He kept coming closer and closer, all twisted and epileptic, without a rib in his body.

"Pole's coming at you, but you ain't coming at the Pole..." the Cossack muttered, twitching and shifting his shattered hip. "Where's the reason for that?..."

"Pole's coming at me," I answered boldly, "but I ain't coming at the Pole..."

"So you're a Molokan[1] then?" Akinfiyev whispered, stepping back.

"So I'm a Molokan," I said, louder than before. "Whaddya want, Ivan?"

"What I want is for you to know it," Ivan shouted with wild triumph. "For you to know it, and I got me a written law about Molokans—law says you can shoot 'em down, the God-worshippers…"

The Cossack kept shouting about Molokans, gathering a crowd. I started to walk away from him, but he caught up with me and hit me on the back with his fist.

"You didn't load no cartridges," Akinfiyev whispered haltingly, right into my ear, and set to work, trying to tear my mouth open with his thumbs. "You worship God, traitor…"

He tugged and tore at my mouth; I was pushing the epileptic away, punching him in the face. Akinfiyev fell to the ground sideways and busted himself bloody.

Then Sashka went over to him with her dangling breasts. The woman doused Ivan with water and pulled from his mouth a long tooth, which had been swaying in that black hole like a birch on a bare road.

"Cocks have only got one care in the world," said Sashka, "and that's knocking their beaks together, but me—today's business makes me wanna cover me eyes…"

She said this mournfully and led the shattered Akinfiyev off with her, while I trudged into the village of Cześniki, which had slipped on the tireless Galician rain.

The village floated and swelled, crimson clay flowing from its dismal wounds. The first star sparkled above me and plunged into the clouds. Rain lashed at the willows and grew weary. Evening flew up into the sky like a flock of birds, and darkness lowered its wet wreath onto my head. Dead tired and stooping beneath my funereal crown, I walked on, begging fate for the simplest of knacks—the knack of killing a man.

*Galicia, September 1920*

# SONG

IN THE HAMLET of Budziatycze it fell to my lot to be billeted with a bad hostess. She was a widow, poor; I busted many locks on her larders but found no poultry.

So I had to be clever about it, and one day, after returning home early, before dusk, I saw the hostess shutting the door on her oven, which was still warm. There was a smell of *shchi* in the hut, and there could've been meat in that *shchi*. I scented meat in her *shchi* and laid my revolver on the table, but the old woman denied it. Spasms showed in her face and black fingers; she darkened all over and looked at me with fear and astounding hatred. But nothing would've saved her—I'd have gotten it out of her with my revolver, had I not been interrupted by Sashka Konyayev, otherwise known as Sashka the Christ.

He walked into the hut with an accordion under his arm, his splendid legs knocking about in broken-down boots.

"Let's play us some songs," he said, and looked up at me with eyes full of sleepy blue ice. "Let's play us some songs," Sashka said, sitting down on a bench, and played a little prelude.

It was as if this pensive prelude were drifting in from afar; the Cossack cut it off and his blue eyes grew glum. He turned away from us and, knowing how to please me, struck up a song from the Kuban.

"Star of the fields," he sang, "star of the fields above my father's house, my mother's mournful hand…"

I loved that song—the love of it raised my heart to a state of sublime ecstasy. Sashka knew this, because both of us, he and I, first heard it in 1919, in the Don delta, near the Cossack village of Kagalnitskaya.

A hunter who plied his trade in protected waters taught us the song. Those protected waters are swarming with spawning fish, with countless flocks of birds. The fish propagate in ineffable abundance, so that you can scoop them up with buckets or just with your hands, and if you put an oar in the water, it'll stand upright—the fish will hold it, carry it off with them. We saw it for ourselves; we'll never forget the protected waters near Kagalnitskaya. All the authorities prohibited hunting there—this is a proper prohibition—but there was a brutal war in the delta in 1919, and the hunter Yakov, who plied his improper trade right in front of us, gave Sashka the Christ, our squadron's singer, an accordion so that we'd turn a blind eye. He taught Sashka his songs; many of them were ancient heartfelt chants. And so we forgave the crafty hunter everything, because we needed his songs: back then, no one could see an end to the war, and Sashka alone paved our wearisome path with jangling and tears. A bloody trail stretched along this path. Songs hovered above our trail. So it was in the Kuban and in the Green campaigns,[1] so it was in Uralsk and in the foothills of the Caucasus, and so it is to this day. We need songs, no one sees an end to the war, and Sashka the Christ, the squadron's singer, isn't ripe for death…

And this evening too, when I'd been cheated of my hostess's *shchi*, Sashka pacified me with his half-stifled, swaying voice.

"Star of the fields," he sang, "star of the fields above my father's house, my mother's mournful hand…"

And I listened to him, stretched out on my fusty bedding in the corner. Reverie broke my bones, reverie shook the rotten hay beneath me; through its torrid downpour I could barely make out the old woman propping her withered cheek on her hand. She stood near the wall without stirring, her insect-bitten head drooping, and didn't budge after Sashka had finished playing. Sashka finished and put aside the accordion; he yawned and laughed, as after a long sleep, and then, noticing the desolation of our widow's cabin, brushed the dirt from the bench and brought a bucket of water into the hut.

"You see, sweetheart," the hostess said to him, scratched her back against the door and pointed to me, "your chief there showed up just now, shouted at me, stamped about, took all the locks off my house and laid his gun out for me… It's a sin from God, laying a gun out for me—I'm a woman, you know…"

She scratched against the door again and began throwing sheepskins over her son. Her son was snoring under the icon on a big bed strewn with rags. He was a mute boy with a waterlogged, swollen white head and the giant feet of a grown peasant. His mother wiped his dirty nose and returned to the table.

"Hostess," Sashka said then and touched her shoulder. "If you'd like, I can show you a little attention…"

But it was as if the old woman hadn't heard his words.

"Haven't seen any *shchi*," she said, propping her cheek. "My *shchi*'s all gone, and all people do is show me their guns, and if I come across a good fellow and it's time for a little sweetness, well, I'm so sick to my stomach, I can't even get joy outta sinning…"

She dragged out her dismal complaints and, muttering, pushed the mute boy closer to the wall. Sashka lay down with her on the rag-covered bed, while I tried to fall asleep and began thinking up dreams, so as to fall asleep with good thoughts.

## THE REBBE'S SON

...DO YOU REMEMBER ZHITOMIR, Vasily? Do you remember the Teterev River, Vasily, and that night when the Sabbath, the youthful Sabbath, came slinking across the sunset, pressing the stars down with her little red heel?

The moon's slender horn bathed its arrows in the Teterev's black water. Silly Gedali, founder of the Fourth International, led us to Rebbe Motale Bratslavsky's for the evening prayers. The cock feathers on silly Gedali's top hat swayed in the red smoke of the evening. The predatory pupils of candles flickered in the rebbe's room. Broad-shouldered Jews moaned dully, bent over their prayer books, and the old fool of the Chernobyl *tsaddik*s jingled copper coins in his tattered pocket...

...Do you remember that night, Vasily?... Outside the window horses neighed and Cossacks shouted. The wasteland of war gaped outside the window, and Rebbe Motale Bratslavsky, digging his withered fingers into his *tallit*, prayed at the eastern wall. Then the curtain of the Ark parted, and in the candles' funereal splendour we saw the scrolls of the Torah, wrapped in a cover of purple velvet and light-blue silk, and over the Torah hung the lifeless, obedient, beautiful face of Ilya, the rebbe's son, the last prince of the dynasty...

Well, two days ago, Vasily, the regiments of the Twelfth Army opened the front at Kovel. The conqueror's scornful cannonade thundered over the city. Our troops wavered and got mixed up. The political-department train took off, creeping across the dead backbone of the fields. And monstrous Russia, as improbable as a flock of clothing lice, went stamping in bast shoes along both sides of the carriages. The typhoid-ridden peasantry rolled before it the customary hump of a soldier's death. It jumped up onto our train's footboards and fell away, knocked down by rifle butts. It snorted, scrabbled, rushed forward and kept silent. And at the twelfth *verst*, when I'd run out of potatoes, I hurled a pile of Trotsky's leaflets at them. But only one man reached for a leaflet with a dirty, dead hand. And I recognized Ilya, the son of the Zhitomir rebbe. I recognized him right off, Vasily. And it was so agonizing to see a prince who'd lost his trousers, who'd been bent in two by a soldier's knapsack, that we broke regulations and pulled him into the carriage. Bare knees, clumsy as an old woman's, knocked against the rusty iron of the steps; two big-breasted typists in sailors' jackets dragged the dying man's long, shy body along the floor. We laid him in a corner on the floor of the editorial office. Cossacks in red trousers straightened his clothes, which had slipped off. The girls, standing firm on the bowed legs of unpretentious cows, coldly observed his sexual parts—the wilted, tender, curly-haired manhood of a worn-out Semite. While I, who had seen him on one of my nights of wandering—I started packing a little trunk with the scattered belongings of Red Army soldier Bratslavsky.

Everything was thrown together in one heap—the mandates of the agitator and the commemorative booklets of a Jewish poet. The portraits of Lenin and Maimonides lay side by side. The knotted iron of Lenin's skull and the dull silk of Maimonides's portraits. A lock of woman's hair was pressed in a book of resolutions from the Sixth Party Congress, and the margins of communist leaflets were crammed with the crooked lines of Ancient Hebrew verse. They fell upon me in a scarce, sorrowful rain—a page from the Song of Songs and the cartridges from a revolver. The sorrowful rain of sunset washed the dust from my hair, and I said to the boy dying in the corner on a tattered mattress:

"Four months ago, on a Friday evening, the junkman Gedali brought me to your father, Rebbe Motale, but you weren't in the Party back then, Bratslavsky."

"I was in the Party back then," said the boy, clawing at his chest and writhing in his fever, "but I couldn't leave my mother…"

"And now, Ilya?"

"In the revolution, my mother's an episode," he whispered, quieting down. "My letter came up, the letter B, and the organization sent me to the front…"

"And you wound up in Kovel, Ilya?"

"I wound up in Kovel!" he cried in despair. "The *kulak*[1] bastards opened the front. I took over a scratch regiment, but too late. Didn't have the artillery…"

\*

He died before reaching Rovno. He died, the last prince, among poems, phylacteries and foot cloths. We buried him at some forgotten station. And I—barely able to contain the tempests of my imagination inside my ancient body—I received my brother's final breath.

# POSTSCRIPT

## (1933)

# ARGAMAK

I DECIDED TO GO to the front. The division commander winced at the news.

"Where you rushing off to?... You'll stand and gape—they'll nip you in the bud..."

I insisted. And that's not all. My choice fell on the division that saw the most action—the Sixth. I was assigned to the Fourth Squadron of the Twenty-Third Cavalry Regiment. The squadron was commanded by a metalworker of the Bryansk factory named Baulin, a boy in years. He grew out a beard as a warning. Ashen tufts curled on his chin. In his twenty-two years Baulin had let nothing unnerve him. This quality, inherent to thousands of Baulins, served as an important component in the victory of the revolution. Baulin was tough, taciturn, stubborn. His path in life was decided. He never doubted the correctness of this path. Privation came easy to him. He could sleep sitting up. He slept with one hand clutching the other, and woke up in such a way that the transition from slumber to wakefulness was imperceptible.

You could expect no mercy under Baulin's command. My service began with a rare omen of good fortune—I was given a horse. There were no reserve horses, no horses among the peasants. Chance came to the rescue. The Cossack Tikhomolov killed two captive officers without permission. He was ordered to accompany them to brigade headquarters; the officers might've had important information to give. Tikhomolov didn't bring them all the way. They decided to try the Cossack before the Revolutionary Tribunal, then changed their minds. Squadron Commander Baulin imposed a punishment more terrible than the tribunal—he confiscated Tikhomolov's stallion, who was called Argamak, and sent the Cossack to the unit transport.

The torment I went through with Argamak nearly surpassed the limits of human strength. Tikhomolov had brought the horse from the Terek, from home. It was trained for the Cossack trot, that peculiar Cossack gallop—dry, furious, sudden. Argamak's stride was long, extended, stubborn. With this diabolical stride he'd carry me out of the ranks; I'd fall away from the squadron and, losing my orientation, would wander for days in search of my unit, wind up behind enemy lines, sleep in the ravines, sidle up to other regiments and get chased away. My cavalry know-how was limited to having served in the artillery battalion of the Fifteenth Infantry Division during the German War. Most of the time I sat enthroned on an ammunition cart; every now and then we'd ride in gun teams. There was no place for me to get used to Argamak's stiff, staggering trot. Tikhomolov had bequeathed to his horse all the devils of his downfall. I shook like a sack on the stallion's long, dry back. I wore out his back. It broke out in sores. Metallic flies ate away at these sores. Hoops of clotted black blood girded the horse's belly. Inept shoeing made Argamak overreach, and his hind legs swelled in the fetlock joint, becoming elephantine. Argamak was wasting away. His eyes were shot with a fire peculiar to the tormented horse—the fire of hysteria and perseverance. He wouldn't let himself be saddled.

"You abolished that horse, four-eyes," said the platoon commander.

The Cossacks kept silent around me; they were readying themselves behind my back, as predators do, in drowsy and treacherous stillness. They didn't even ask me to write their letters any more…

The Cavalry Army took Novograd-Volynsk. We had to cover sixty, eighty kilometres each day and night. We were nearing Rovno. Our day rests were pitiful. Night after night I dreamt the same dream. I'm racing along at a trot on Argamak. Bonfires line the road. Cossacks are cooking their food. I ride past them, and they don't raise their eyes. Some greet me, others don't even look—I'm of no concern. What does this mean? Their indifference signifies that there's nothing special in my manner of riding; I ride like everyone else, and there's no point in looking at me. I gallop on my way and am happy. My thirst for peace and happiness wasn't quenched during waking hours, and so I dreamt dreams.

Tikhomolov was nowhere to be seen. He kept watch over me from somewhere on the fringes of the march, from its sluggish tail end of carts crammed with rags.

The platoon commander once said to me:

"Pashka keeps asking after you, how you're faring…"

"What's he need me for?"

"Seems he needs you…"

"He thinks I did him wrong, is that it?"

"You're saying you didn't?…"

Pashka's hatred reached me through woods and rivers. I felt it on my skin and shivered. His bloodshot eyes were glued to my path.

"Why'd you give me an enemy?" I asked Baulin.

The squadron commander rode past and yawned.

"That's not my grief," he said without looking back. "That's your grief…"

Argamak's back would heal, then open up again. I'd put no fewer than three cloths under the saddle, but I couldn't ride properly, and the weals wouldn't close. The knowledge that I was sitting on an open wound kept nagging at me.

One of the Cossacks from our platoon, Bizyukov by name, was a countryman of Tikhomolov's. He knew Pashka's father there, on the Terek.

"So Pashka's old man," Bizyukov told me once, "he likes breeding horses… Gutsy rider, that one, stout… He comes to see a herd—gonna pick out a horse… They bring one out. He plants himself right in front of it, feet apart, looks straight at it… Whaddya need?… Here's what he needs: he swings his fist, gives it to 'im right between the eyes—no more horse. Why'd you do it, Kalistrat—kill off the animal?… That horse ain't to my terrible liking… Didn't take a liking to that horse, wouldn't ride… My liking, he says, is a deadly thing… Gutsy rider, that one, that's for sure."

And so Argamak, whom Pashka's father had left alive, whom he'd chosen, had ended up in my hands. What was I going to do? I turned over countless plans in my mind. War saved me from my worries.

The Cavalry Army attacked Rovno. The city was taken. We stayed there two days. The next night the Poles drove us out. They gave battle so as to let their retreating units pass through. The manoeuvre worked. The Poles had a hurricane for cover—lashing rain, a heavy summer storm that toppled onto the world in streams of black water. We evacuated the city for a day. The Serb Dundić, the bravest of men, fell in this night-time battle.[1] Pashka Tikhomolov fought in this battle too. The Poles swooped down on his transport. The field was flat, without any cover. Pashka arranged his wagons in a battle formation that he alone knew. This must have been how the Romans arranged their chariots. It turns out Pashka had a machine gun. One has to assume he stole it and hid it away just in case. With this machine gun Tikhomolov fought off the assault, saved our property and led out the whole transport, with the exception of two carts whose horses had been shot.

"Keeping your fighters on ice?" they asked Baulin at brigade headquarters a few days after the battle.

"If I am, I must have my reasons…"

"Watch yourself, or you'll get it…"

Pashka hadn't been granted a pardon, but we knew he'd be coming. He came wearing galoshes on his bare feet. His fingers had been chopped off, and ribbons of black gauze hung down from them. The ribbons trailed behind him like a mantle. Pashka came to the village of Budziatycze, to the square in front of the Catholic church, where our horses stood tethered to the hitching post. Baulin was sitting on the church steps, steaming his feet in a tub. His toes had started to rot. They were pink—the pink of iron when the tempering has just begun. Tufts of youthful straw hair stuck to Baulin's forehead. The sun shone on the bricks and tiles of the church. Bizyukov, who was standing next to Baulin, stuck a cigarette in the squadron commander's mouth and lit it. Tikhomolov, trailing his tattered mantle, went over to the hitching post. His galoshes flopped. Argamak stretched out his long neck and whinnied at his owner—whinnied softly and shrilly, like a horse in the desert. Ichor twisted like lace on his back between strips of torn flesh. Pashka stood beside the horse. The dirty ribbons lay motionless on the ground.

"So that's how it is," the Cossack pronounced, almost inaudibly.

I stepped forward.

"Let's make peace, Pashka. I'm glad the horse is going to you. I can't cope with him… Let's make peace, all right?…"

"It's not Easter, yet, to be making peace," the platoon commander said, rolling a cigarette behind my back. His Cossack trousers were loosened, his shirt unbuttoned over his copper chest; he was resting on the church steps.

"Give 'im three Easter kisses, Pashka," muttered Bizyukov, Tikhomolov's countryman, who knew Pashka's father, Kalistrat. "He wants three kisses..."

I was alone among these people, whose friendship I had failed to win.

Pashka stood in front of the horse as if rooted to the spot. Argamak, breathing strongly and freely, stretched his muzzle towards him.

"So that's how it is," the Cossack repeated, turned sharply towards me and said steadily: "I won't be making peace with you."

Shuffling with his galoshes, he started off down the chalky, scorched road, sweeping the dust of the village square with his bandages. Argamak followed him like a dog. The reins swayed beneath his muzzle and his long neck hung low. Baulin kept rubbing the reddish, iron-coloured rot of his feet in the tub.

"You've given me an enemy," I said to him. "But how's any of this my fault?"

The squadron commander raised his head.

"I see you," he said. "I see you through and through... Aiming to live without enemies... That's all you want—no enemies..."

"Give 'im three kisses," Bizyukov muttered, turning away.

A fiery patch appeared on Baulin's forehead. His cheek twitched.

"You know what you get that way?" he said, unable to control his breathing. "What you get is boredom... Shove off back to your goddam mother..."

So I had to leave. I transferred to the Sixth Squadron. Things went better there. Despite everything, Argamak had taught me Tikhomolov's manner of riding. Months passed. My dream came true. The Cossacks stopped following me and my horse with their eyes.

*1924–30*

# APPENDIX: TOPONYMS

| Eastern and Central Europe | Current Name and Location | Nineteenth-Century Imperial Affiliation |
|---|---|---|
| BELAYA TSERKOV | *Bila Tserkva*, Ukraine | Russia |
| BELYOV | *Biliv*, Ukraine | Russia |
| BERESTECHKO (BERESTECZKO) | *Berestechko*, Ukraine | Russia |
| BREST | *Brest*, Belarus | Russia |
| BRODY | *Brody*, Ukraine | Austria |
| BUDZIATYCZE | *Budyatychi*, Ukraine | Austria |
| BUSK | *Busk*, Ukraine | Russia |
| CHERNOBYL | *Chernobyl* or *Chornobyl*, Ukraine | Russia |
| CRACOW | *Kraków*, Poland | Austria, Duchy of Warsaw, Free City of Kraków |
| CZEŚNIKI | *Cześniki*, Poland | Austria |
| DUBNO | *Dubno*, Ukraine | Austria |
| FASTOV | *Fastiv*, Ukraine | Russia |
| HUSIATYN | *Husiatyn*, Ukraine | Austria |

| Eastern and Central Europe | Current Name and Location | Nineteenth-Century Imperial Affiliation |
| --- | --- | --- |
| KHOTIN | *Khotyn*, Ukraine | Ottoman Empire, Russia |
| KLEKOTÓW | *Klekotiv*, Ukraine | Austria |
| KOVEL | *Kovel*, Ukraine | Russia |
| KOZIN | *Kozyn*, Ukraine | Russia |
| KRAPIVNO | *Kropyvnya*, Ukraine | Russia |
| KREMENETS | *Kremenets*, Ukraine | Russia |
| LUBLIN | *Lublin*, Poland | Austria |
| LWÓW | *Lviv*, Ukraine | Austria |
| NOVOGRAD-VOLYNSK | *Novohrad-Volynskyi*, Ukraine | Russia |
| ODESSA | *Odessa*, Ukraine | Russia |
| OSTROPOL | *Ostropol*, Ukraine | Russia |
| RADZIECHÓW | *Radekhiv*, Ukraine | Austria |
| RADZIVILOV | *Radyvyliv*, Ukraine | Russia |
| ROVNO | *Rivne*, Ukraine | Russia |
| SITANIEC | *Sitaniec*, Poland | Austria |
| SOKAL | *Sokal*, Ukraine | Austria |
| VILNA | *Vilnius*, Lithuania | Russia |
| VITEBSK | *Vitebsk*, *Vitsebsk* or *Viciebsk*, Belarus | Russia |
| WARSAW | *Warszawa*, Poland | Prussia, Duchy of Warsaw, Congress Poland, Russia |
| ZAMOŚĆ | *Zamość*, Poland | Austria |
| ZHITOMIR | *Zhytomyr*, Ukraine | Russia |

## RUSSIAN CITIES

*General's Bridge* (now *Generalskoye*), Rodionovo-Nesvetaysky District, Rostov Oblast

*Grozny*, Chechen Republic

*Kagalnitskaya*, Kagalnitsky District, Rostov Oblast

*Kasimov*, Ryazan Oblast

*Kastornaya* (now *Kastornoye*), Kastorensky District, Kursk Oblast

*Krasnodar*, Krasnodar Krai

*Maykop*, Republic of Adygea

*Mozhaysk*, Mozhaysky District, Moscow Oblast

*Nizhny Novgorod* (often shortened to *Nizhny*; between 1932 and 1990, *Gorky*), Nizhny Novgorod Oblast

*Novorossiysk*, Krasnodar Krai

*Platovskaya*, Proletarsky District, Rostov Oblast

*Prikumsk* (before 1921, *Svyatoy Krest* [*Holy Cross*]; since 1935, *Budyonnovsk*), Stavropol Krai

*Rostov*, Yaroslavl Oblast

*Ryazan*, Ryazan Oblast

*Shuya*, Ivanovo Oblast

*Tambov*, Tambov Oblast

*Temryuk*, Temryuksky District, Krasnodar Krai

*Tsaritsyn* (renamed *Stalingrad* in 1925; since 1961, *Volgograd*), Volgograd Oblast

*Uralsk* (after 1991, *Oral*), Kazakhstan

*Voronezh*, Voronezh Oblast

## REGIONS

*Krasnodar Region (Krai)*, Russia

*Kuban*, Russia

*Stavropol Region (Krai)*, Russia

*Galicia / Halychyna / Galicja*, Ukraine and Poland

*Volyn / Volhynia*, Ukraine, Poland, and Belarus

## RIVERS

*Bug (Western Bug or Buh)*, Poland, Belarus and Ukraine

*Don*, Russia

*Donets (Seversky Donets)*, Russia and Ukraine

*Terek*, Georgia and Russia

*Teterev* (now *Teteriv*), Ukraine

*Volga*, Russia

*Zbrucz* (now *Zbruch*), Ukraine

# NOTES

## CROSSING THE ZBRUCZ

1 Pan: a Western Slavic honorific, also used in Ukraine and Belarus, meaning "lord" or "master" and roughly equivalent to "sir" or "mister" in usage. The female equivalent is Pani.

## THE CATHOLIC CHURCH IN NOVOGRAD

1 The Polish-Lithuanian Commonwealth, established at the Union of Lublin in July 1569, was one of the largest and most populous states in Europe in the sixteenth and seventeenth centuries, but it entered a period of decline in the eighteenth century and was wiped off the map in 1795, after the Third Partition by the monarchs of Russia, Prussia and Austria. Poland ceased to exist as a state until independence was once again declared on 11 November 1918 by Józef Piłsudski (1867–1935), who remained the country's leader until 1935.

2 The Radziwiłłs and Sapiehas were among the most powerful princely families in the Commonwealth. Princes Janusz Radziwiłł (1880–1967) and Eustachy Sapieha (1881–1963) were members of Piłsudski's government; Sapieha served in the Polish cavalry

during the Polish–Soviet War. The town of Radzivilov, mentioned repeatedly throughout the cycle, is named after a member of the Radziwiłł family.

## A LETTER

1   Though not a Cossack himself, Semyon Mikhaylovich Budyonny (1883–1973) was born and raised among the Don Cossacks of the Rostov region. He was drafted into the Imperial Army in 1903, became a cavalryman and served in the Russo-Japanese War. He became a cavalry officer in 1908 and served with distinction in the First World War, although he had repeated trouble with his superiors. He sided with the Bolsheviks after the October Revolution of 1917 and formed a Red Cavalry detachment in the Don region, which became the First Cavalry Army in 1919. He fought at Tsaritsyn and Voronezh, where he became a close associate of Kliment Voroshilov and Joseph Stalin (see note on Voroshilov on p. 213). After the Civil War, Budyonny's status climbed steadily; he was named a Marshal of the Soviet Union in 1935. Although Stalin relieved him of his duty as Commander-in-Chief of the south-western and southern fronts during the Second World War, Budyonny remained in the leadership's good graces and was named a Hero of the Soviet Union in 1958, 1963 and 1968.

2   General Anton Ivanovich Denikin (1872–1947) was one of the leaders of the anti-Bolshevik White movement in the Russian Civil War. He commanded the White forces in southern Russia.

3   *verst*: an obsolete Russian unit of measure, equivalent to 3,500 feet or approximately one kilometre.

## PAN APOLEK

1 *zrazy*: stuffed meat cutlets, eaten throughout Eastern Europe.

2 *Oj, ten człowiek!*: "Oh, that man!" (Polish).

3 *Co wy mówicie?*: "What are you saying?" (Polish).

4 *Tak, tak... Panie*: "Yes, yes... yes, yes, sir..." (Polish).

## THE ITALIAN SUN

1 Nestor Ivanovych Makhno, called "Old Man" (1888–1934), was a Ukrainian anarcho-communist who commanded his own independent Revolutionary Insurrectionary Army of Ukraine during the Civil War. Volin—or Voline, as he himself spelt it—was the *nom de guerre* of Vsevolod Mikhaylovich Eikhenbaum (1882–1945), a prominent Russian Jewish anarchist who collaborated with Makhno, helped organize his army and wrote many of his manifestos. Both Makhno and Volin were driven into exile in 1921.

2 "*Tsek*" is Sidorov's corruption of the abbreviation TsK (pronounced "tse-ka")—which stands for Central Committee, the chief administrative body of the Communist Party. "*Tsekist*" is a member of the Central Committee. Later in the letter, Sidorov uses the correct form of the abbreviation (*Tseka*), and also refers to the *Cheka*, the secret police, itself an acronym (ChK) for Emergency Commission.

## MY FIRST GOOSE

1 The character of Savitsky is based on Semyon Konstantinovich Timoshenko (1895–1970), the son of a Ukrainian peasant from what is now the Odessa region, who was drafted into the Imperial

Army in 1914 and joined the Red Army in 1918. He commanded the Sixth Division from November 1919 to August 1920; he was wounded five times during the Civil War and the Polish conflict. He had participated in the defence of Tsaritsyn (see note on Voroshilov on p. 213), where he befriended Semyon Budyonny and Joseph Stalin. Timoshenko rose to become a People's Commissar for Defence and a Marshal of the Soviet Union in 1940. His daughter married Stalin's son in 1944. After commanding troops on various fronts during the Second World War, Timoshenko became Inspector-General of the Defence Ministry.

## THE REBBE

1 Hershel of Ostropol is a trickster figure in Yiddish folklore.

2 *tsaddik*: a term of respect in the Jewish tradition, bestowed upon the most righteous figures.

## THE TACHANKA DOCTRINE

1 *tachanka*: a machine-gun cart.

2 *britchka*: a long horse-drawn carriage.

## THE SECOND BRIGADE COMMANDER

1 *koleso*: wheel (Russian).

2 *sazhen*: an obsolete Russian unit of measure, equivalent to seven feet, or approximately two metres.

3 Vasily Ivanovich Kniga (1883–1961) was a Soviet military commander, who would be become a major general in 1940. He began

his career as a cavalry officer in the First World War, and joined the Red Army soon after the October Revolution. During the Civil War he commanded the Thirty-First Cavalry Regiment of the First Stavropol Cavalry Division and the First Cavalry Brigade of the First Cavalry Army's Sixth Cavalry Division. He was a native of Stavropol, and a close associate of Iosif Apanasenko (see note on Pavlichenko below) and Konstantin Arkhipov Trunov (1866–1920), the subject of the story 'Squadron Commander Trunov' (p. 132).

### SASHKA THE CHRIST

1  *pood* and *desyatina*: obsolete Russian units of measure, the first being roughly equivalent to thirty-six pounds (sixteen kilograms), and the second to 11,000 square metres (118,000 square feet).

2  Kliment Yefremovich Voroshilov (1881–1969) led the defence of Tsaritsyn, commanded the Tenth and Fourteenth Armies, and was one of the organizers of Budyonny's First Cavalry during the Russian Civil War and the Polish–Soviet War. He was a close associate of Joseph Stalin and served as People's Commissar for Military and Naval Affairs and Chairman of the Revolutionary Military Council of the USSR from 1925 to 1934, as People's Commissar for Defence from 1934 to 1940 and, in 1935, was named a Marshal of the Soviet Union.

### THE LIFE STORY OF PAVLICHENKO, MATVEI RODIONYCH

1  The character of Pavlichenko is based on Iosif Rodionovich Apanasenko (1890–1943), who had indeed been a herdsman in

Stavropol before being drafted into the Imperial Army in 1911. He commanded the Sixth Division from August to October 1920. Apanasenko rose through the ranks in the interwar years and was killed at the front in 1943, to which he had been sent after repeatedly lobbying for reassignment to active duty.

## THE CEMETERY IN KOZIN

1   Bohdan Khmelnytsky (*c.*1595—1657) was a hetman of the Zaporozhian Host of Cossacks in the Polish–Lithuanian Commonwealth. He led an uprising that resulted in the creation of an independent Cossack state. The Treaty of Pereyaslav, which he concluded with the Tsardom of Russia in 1654, led to the eventual absorption of this state into the Russian Empire; there is a controversy as to how the signatories interpreted the terms of the treaty. Khmelnytsky's uprising devastated the Jewish community of the Commonwealth.

## KONKIN

1   "Checking his papers" is a euphemism for execution or shooting at close range. Nikolai Nikolayevich Dukhonin (1876–1917) was the last commander-in-chief of the Russian Imperial Army after Kerensky's flight. He surrendered to the Bolsheviks but was bayoneted to death by a mob of soldiers and sailors, who then used his body for target practice.

2   *Nie moge, Pan*: "I can't, Pan" (Polish).

## BERESTECHKO

1 *Berestetchko… sept semaines*: "Berestechko, 1820. Paul, my beloved, they say the Emperor Napoleon is dead, is this true? I'm well, the birth was easy, our little hero is already seven weeks old" (French).

## EVENING

1 Nicholas the Bloody refers to Nicholas II, the last tsar of the Romanov dynasty, who was executed by the Bolsheviks in Yekaterinburg in 1918; Peter III was murdered in 1762 by the Orlov brothers, who conspired with his wife, who would become Catherine II, the Great; Paul was Catherine's son and was murdered by courtiers in 1801; Nicholas I, who was nicknamed "the Rod" for introducing harsh corporal punishment into the Imperial Army, was rumoured to have poisoned himself, depressed by the army's losses in the Crimean War; Nicholas's son Alexander II was assassinated by populist terrorists in 1881; Alexander's son Alexander III was rumoured to have been an alcoholic.

## AFONKA BIDA

1 *ataman*: Cossack chieftain. The origins of this term are disputed. It may derive from the German *Hauptmann*, via Polish *hetman*, meaning "captain", or from the Turkish *ataman*, meaning "father of horsemen".

2 Maslyakov: First Brigade commander of the Fourth Division, an incorrigible partisan who would soon betray Soviet power [author's note].

IN ST VALENTINE'S

1 *kontusz* (Polish spelling): a long outer garment worn by Polish, Lithuanian, Belarusian and Ukrainian nobility, as well as by Ukrainian Cossacks, in the time of the Polish–Lithuanian Commonwealth.

SQUADRON COMMANDER TRUNOV

1 Gaon: a term of respect used for great sages in the Jewish tradition. Elijah ben Shlomo Zalman Kremer (1720–97), known as the Vilna (Vilnius) Gaon, was a Talmudist and Kabbalist who opposed the movement of Hasidism, which was founded by Israel ben Eliezer (1698–1760), known as the Baal Shem Tov. Husiatyn was the seat of an important dynasty of Hasidic rebbes.

2 Cedric Fauntleroy (or Faunt le Roy) (1891–1973) was an American First World War flying ace who volunteered to serve in the Polish Air Force during the Polish–Soviet War, joining the Polish Seventh Air Escadrille. He took command of the escadrille in 1919. Made up mostly of American volunteer pilots, the escadrille became known as the Kościuszko Squadron, in honour of Tadeusz Kościuszko (1746–1817), who fought on the American side in the American Revolutionary War and, as supreme commander of the Polish National Armed Forces, led the Poles' unsuccessful uprising against the Russian Empire in 1794. The narrator later mistakenly refers to Major Fauntleroy as Reginald, not Cedric.

## THE IVANS

1 Sergei Sergeyevich Kamenev (1881–1936) was an important Soviet military leader; during the Civil War he served as commander of the Eastern Front from 1918 to 1919, and commander-in-chief of the Armed Forces of the republic from 1919 to 1924.

2 A syringe for the treatment of syphilis, named after the Russian venerologist V.M. Tarnovsky (1837–1906).

## THE WIDOW

1 Boris Viktorovich Savinkov (1879–1925) was one of the leaders of the Russian Socialist Revolutionary Party, a political organization responsible for a campaign of assassinations of imperial officials at the turn of the twentieth century. After the February Revolution of 1917, he served as Deputy War Minister in the provisional government, but he soon resigned from the post and was expelled from the SRs for supporting an anti-government uprising. After the October Revolution, Savinkov led several failed uprisings against the Bolsheviks before emigrating to France. During the Polish–Soviet War he moved to Poland, forming cavalry and infantry units of Red Army POWs who were willing to switch sides and fight against the Soviet forces; after the war ended, he was expelled from Poland. He was captured while attempting to infiltrate the USSR in 1924 and died in the custody of the secret police.

## ZAMOŚĆ

1 *Nic nie ma*: "There's nothing" (Polish).

2 *Czekaj!*: "Wait!" (Polish).

## AFTER THE BATTLE

1 Molokans, or "milk-drinkers", are members of a pacifist Christian sect who broke away from the Russian Orthodox Church; their name is thought to derive from their practice of drinking milk on fasting days, when Orthodox Christians are prohibited from consuming meat and dairy.

## SONG

1 The Green armies were groups of peasants who took up arms against all the governments involved in the Russian Civil War of 1917–22 in order to protect their interests.

## THE REBBE'S SON

1 The *kulak* (Russian: literally, "fist") is a rich peasant. They were traditional enemies of the Bolsheviks and were virtually eliminated during the mass collectivization of the countryside in the 1920s and 1930s.

## ARGAMAK

1 Aleksa Dundić (1896 or 1897–1920) was most likely a Croat, not a Serb. He was recruited into the Austro-Hungarian Army during

the First World War, taken prisoner by the Russian Imperial Army in 1916 and volunteered to fight on the Russian side in the Serbian Volunteer Corps. He joined the Red Army in 1917 and participated in the defence of Tsaritsyn with Voroshilov in 1918. He joined Budyonny's troops in 1919, and was deeply admired by his fellow cavalrymen for his courage and skill. He fell at the Battle of Rovno, as described in this story, on 8 July 1920.

# Pushkin Press

Pushkin Press was founded in 1997, and publishes novels, essays, memoirs, children's books—everything from timeless classics to the urgent and contemporary.

This book is part of the Pushkin Collection of paperbacks, designed to be as satisfying as possible to hold and to enjoy. It is typeset in Monotype Baskerville, based on the transitional English serif typeface designed in the mid-eighteenth century by John Baskerville. It was litho-printed on Munken Premium White Paper and notch-bound by the independently owned printer TJ International in Padstow, Cornwall. The cover, with French flaps, was printed on Colorplan Pristine White paper. The paper and cover board are both acid-free and Forest Stewardship Council (FSC) certified.

Pushkin Press publishes the best writing from around the world—great stories, beautifully produced, to be read and read again.